PRAISE FOR VIVIAN AREND

"If you've never read a Vivian Arend book you are missing out on one of the best contemporary authors writing today."
~ *Book Reading Gals*

A Firefighter's Christmas Gift is a sweet romance; a heart-warming and passionate Christmas story. The premise is inspiring and delightful: the romance is encouraging and sensual.
~The Reading Cafe

This is a wonderful love story, and it was a magical Christmas story. It was great to celebrate the holiday with the residents of heart falls.
~ Book Addict Live

WITHDRAWN

"This story will keep you reading from the first page to the last one. There is never a dull moment..."
~ *Landy Jimenez*

"I definitely recommend to fans of contemporaries with hot cowboys and strong family ties.."
~ *SmexyBooks*

"This was my first Vivian Arend story, and I know I want more!"
~ *Red Hot Plus Blue Reads*

Another masterpiece of love and passion Ms. Arend and all I have to say is THANK YOU!
~Romance Witch Reviews

ALSO BY VIVIAN AREND

A full list of Vivian's print titles is available on her website

www.vivianarend.com

A COWBOY'S CHRISTMAS LIST

HOLIDAYS IN HEART FALLS: BOOK 4

VIVIAN AREND

A Cowboy's Christmas List
Copyright © 2021 by Arend Publishing Inc.
ISBN: 9781989507407
Edited by Manuela Velasco
Cover Design © Damonza
Proofed by Angie Ramey & Linda Levy

1

$\mathcal{T}$he air surrounding Yvette Wright alternated between comfortable and refreshing, the crisp winter wind sliding over her shoulders every time someone opened the door at the Buns and Roses coffee shop. The last sip of her caramel macchiato lingered on her tongue, sweet yet refreshing. Christmas carols floated on the air, along with the scent of gingerbread and pumpkin spice. In fact, sitting in the coffee shop should have meant blissful perfection.

Nope. Yvette was vibrating so hard that if the chair under her hadn't been absolutely level, she would've rocked a hole in the wooden floor by now.

For the fifth time in under five minutes, she dug the key chain out of her pocket, staring at the small Christmas ornament in her fingers. The shiny golden key on the loop offered no clues whatsoever. The circle of cardboard next to it had begun to fray at the edges because she'd handled it so much since its unexpected arrival in the mail two weeks ago. The note on the circle asked her to be where she was right now.

December 1, Buns and Roses, 12 p.m.

The decorative part of the key chain was a tiny Christmas tree. Small, fake jewels nestled in its branches like a pretend string of lights. It was cute—and appealed to her at a core level.

I swear, you're part magpie.

Her mother's voice echoed in Yvette's mind, a solid memory. The mocking words had always been accompanied by a shake of her head and a click of her tongue.

Yvette's family often complained she was unreasonably attracted to shiny things.

Yet it wasn't the actual key chain making her squirm as if she were a two-year-old during an unending church service. It was very much the thought of *who* had sent the gift.

Alex Thorne. Cowboy at a local ranch, volunteer firefighter coordinator in Heart Falls, and official pain in her butt. Or at least he had been before leaving town months ago, vanishing to his family's farm.

"Keys to the kingdom?" One of Yvette's best friends, Madison Zhao, dropped into the chair opposite her. Her auburn hair lay in two braids over her shoulders, her pale skin flushed from her time in the cold. The green ribbons tied to the ends of her braids were nearly lost amongst the bright and shiny objects sewn all over the tacky red sweater she wore.

Laughing out loud might be rude, but the response was pretty instinctive. Yvette pulled herself together quickly as she blinked at her friend. "Ryan *already* wrangled you into having to wear that monstrosity?"

Tricking each other into wearing the gaudy sweater was a holiday tradition between Madison and her husband, and it appeared that even though Madison was now nearly eight months pregnant, some things would never change. "Ryan informed me he'd finally had time to hang the curtains in the baby's room, so I went to check. He had put them up, but also draped *this* over the curtain rod." She flicked a finger at a fuzzy snowman attached to her left shoulder. "I'm happy he got the ritual rolling so soon, though, because I have such wonderfully evil plans for this year. It'll be his turn to model our famous attire soon enough."

The door to Buns and Roses opened again, and this time, one well-built cowboy slipped in with the cold winter air.

Alex. Worn jeans, a sheepskin-lined jean jacket. Dark-brown cowboy hat on his head, and well-worn leather boots on his feet. The whole cowboy uniform that fit him so well.

After him being gone for most of the year, Yvette expected to discover some change in his appearance. Nope. Same strong jawline, same dark-brown eyes that turned intently in her direction, as if he'd sensed before even opening the door exactly where to find her. His skin was a tanned tone that suggested Mediterranean heritage, his dark hair a bit too long to be considered a military cut.

He headed straight for her as if on a mission.

Madison noticed immediately. She blinked at Yvette in surprise. "Oops. Sorry. Didn't know I was interrupting something."

"You're not," Yvette protested, but Madison shot to her feet so quickly, she wavered.

Before Yvette could move, Alex was there, wrapping an arm around Madison's shoulders and steadying her until she caught her balance.

She offered a smile. "Thanks. Welcome back."

"You're welcome. It's good to be home." Alex's grin widened as his gaze dipped over her. "You're looking well. The sweater suits you. And the bump."

A snort of laughter escaped Madison. She shook a finger at him. "You just wait. You *will* see Ryan wearing this very soon, and it will suit him too, even without a bump."

"Sounds good. I'm back on shift at the fire hall starting tomorrow. If you ever need a hand pulling a fast one..." Alex offered with a wink.

Madison grinned. "I'll keep that in mind." She turned to Yvette and waggled her fingers. "Catch up with you tomorrow. I just stopped to pick up my to-go order of chocolate and fat. Have fun."

Like a whirlwind, Yvette's friend vanished. Which meant the wall of safety she offered vanished as well when Alex pulled out the chair beside Yvette and lowered himself into it.

Those dark eyes drifted over her. She knew the instant he spotted the key ring tucked in her fingers.

His smile widened the slightest bit before he met her gaze again. "Thanks for meeting me."

"Sure."

Suddenly, she didn't know what to do with her hands. Or where to look.

What nonsense. She was a grown woman meeting a man in a public place. She needed to solve a mystery of sorts. Ergo, there was no reason to act like a shy teenager.

Yvette deliberately lifted her gaze and met his square on. "Did you want a coffee?"

"I'll grab it." He flicked a finger at her cup. "Refill?"

"No, thanks."

He was gone before she could ask any more questions.

Yvette distracted herself by glancing around the coffee shop. She exchanged nods with people she'd come to know while working as a veterinarian in Heart Falls over the past two years. She swirled her coffee impatiently. Otherwise, she simply waited.

When Alex returned to the table with his coffee, he also carried a paper bag and a plate covered with cinnamon buns, gingersnaps, and carrot cake. Two of each.

He pushed the tray of treats toward her. "I figured if I asked what you wanted for lunch you'd say *nothing*. But I'm hungry, and I know you like these. Or if you're interested in real food, there're BLTs in here." He shook the bag.

Yvette had to admit his first impulse had been right. Him buying her lunch seemed odd. While she'd been intrigued enough to show up after receiving his strange message, she didn't really consider this a date.

"You certainly know how to make a person curious." Before diving in, though, she needed to ask. "How are your parents?"

Alex sat back, a contented expression crossing his face. "Good. *Really* good, considering they're both in their late seventies and had major surgery. Dad's hip replacement went without a hitch. Glenda had a bit more trouble with her knee surgery, but she's gotten over it. They're both mobile and smart enough to know to behave."

"It was good they had you there to help." The gossip chain had swept through Heart Falls only hours after Alex had packed up and returned home.

He shrugged. "I was lucky to have a boss who let me go on a moment's notice and to still have a job to come back to." Amusement kicked up a notch. "I figured the only way to keep my parents from overdoing it was to sit on them for the first few months. And my sister and her family weren't in any position to help. So I did."

An act of kindness that had floated into Yvette's thoughts far too often, for so many reasons.

None of which had to do with here and now, though. She held up the key chain, letting it dangle from one finger as she spoke. "Want to explain?"

"You know those Advent calendars? The ones where you open a spot every day until Christmas?"

Her brain raced to catch up as she eyed the key. "Those are usually made of cardboard and hide bits of chocolate or different kinds of teas."

"Or wine bottles, or jam, but they were all too one-tone for my purposes."

Which wasn't an answer. She swung the key.

Alex leaned forward, all kidding pushed aside as a very serious, very intent expression replaced it. "I made you a calendar. Every day, you unlock one drawer. Sometimes you'll get to enjoy what's inside on your own, sometimes I want to experience it with you. By the time we hit Christmas, you and I will know each other a lot better. We'll have worked through the bullshit between us, some of which I caused during the past couple of years by acting like a goofy preteen experiencing my first hormone rush."

Yvette pushed aside the bit where he said he'd *made* her a calendar and focused on the part that was the most confusing.

They'd butted heads in the past, that much was true. Even with their disagreements, though, she could honestly say she thought he was a decent person. So was she. It wasn't as if they were archenemies or something that desperately needed fixing. They were oil and water.

So what?

"Why?" Her question seemed to floor him. "I mean, good that you don't want us to fight or get on each other's nerves anymore. That doesn't require you to give me a present."

"Think of it as a charming way for us to become friends. To start dating."

There it was. The point where this suddenly turned very odd. Yvette curled her fingers around the key chain, the solid ridges digging into her palm, warm against her skin.

Alex Thorne wanted to date her.

She met his gaze. The man had never *seemed* the stalker type. "You're not going to pretend that you're in love with me or some such nonsense, are you?"

"Of course not." He stilled. "Although, I should probably admit that I'm pretty sure that I *could* fall in love with you. That's why I think we need to do this."

She stared at him. Her mouth had to be hanging open.

Unperturbed, he continued, "I know a couple who, the

instant they met, he knew they belonged together. It took three years of battling it out before they both admitted it, but still, it was true. They've been a couple for nearly sixty years."

Yvette's ears rang. What on earth could she possibly say? "Um. Congrats to them?"

"I'm not kidding," he insisted. "If I can shortcut three years to one month and save us both a lot of emotional turmoil, it seems like a good idea."

Oh, sweet summer child. "You plan to give me one gift a day until Christmas and, magically, that's going to make the fact we spent nearly two years arguing about everything go away? Alex, we have nothing in common."

"Now you're just being ridiculous," he complained.

Yvette raised a brow. "Not a good way to convince an already-slightly-pissed-off-at-you woman to agree to your hairbrained idea. Just saying."

"Okay, you're right. Although I want to point out we both have jobs that involve ranches and/or animals, which means there's at least *some* common ground between us. We're not complete opposites."

Which was one reason she was still sitting there, listening to this outrageous idea.

She'd been around Alex plenty at Silver Stone ranch. Had even worked beside him, and he'd been wonderful with the animals. Caring, careful, yet just the right amount of firm—

A man animals trusted wasn't all bad.

Although...goats? *Not* the best judge of character, since they themselves were assholes.

She unwrapped her fingers from the key and laid it on the table between them.

"Agree to this, and I promise we will only go as far and fast as you're comfortable. If you ever want more than I'm giving, you just have to ask." Alex met her gaze. "But you need to give dating me a serious try."

She'd been softening, God help her, until his last comment got her back up. "You're exasperating."

"Yes." He grinned. "Is it a deal?"

"Maybe." She couldn't believe she'd just said that. "You really think we're fated mates or something?"

"The fuck? Hell, no. Not unless *you're* secretly turning into a furry creature on a regular basis." His amused expression didn't waver. "And yes, I know what you're talking about. My sister goes through those books like popcorn. Has a whole collection. When I ran out of reading material this past year, I read them too. They're fun and sexy as hell, but if I were able to turn into anything, it would be an eagle or an osprey. Not enough bird-shifter books out there, in my opinion. Guess women don't think cuddling up with someone who gets feathery is hot."

Now Yvette had to fight her own amusement, because she'd actually had that discussion with her girls' night out group before.

Amusement meant she was close to caving. She *was* interested in him, even when he'd been all sorts of a bad idea.

Her thoughts from earlier that day, earlier that week, returned.

She was lonely.

On the friend front, she was good, but she didn't have anyone intimate in her life. She'd had boyfriends before. Even dated a few times during the past year, but each time she'd either called it off in the middle of the first date or he had. Lots of friends, nada on the more.

The *why* that was? She had some suspicions, but actually admitting it, even to herself, was another matter.

Was spending time with Alex really that bad of an idea?

"Okay." She lifted her chin and met his gaze firmly. "As long as you promise that if it's not working for you, however many days there are to go, you call it off. No harm, no foul."

"If you promise the same. Although—we need to clarify

one thing." His expression turned sheepish. "Me being me, and you being you. Arguing, shouting or otherwise being mad at each other for a day or two is not grounds to cancel."

She didn't ask why. "Yeah, well, since you said this was your attempt to shove through three years of bullshit in one month, I hope you're prepared for the high-volume conversations we're sure to enjoy."

His grin was back. "Bring it. Because that also means at some point, when you're ready, we'll have the equivalent of three years of make-up sex to enjoy as well."

Oh, dear Lord.

∾

Alex couldn't stop staring.

While he was doing his best to seem nonchalant about the whole situation, inside he was shaking in his boots. The nervousness would've made him cranky if it weren't for the fact that he'd been dealing with a wide range of emotions every single time Yvette drifted into his mind for pretty much the past year.

First, he'd been annoyed. Felt challenged. Admitting lustful thoughts arose every time he was around her might have been a simple answer, but he didn't want to give in to something simple. Physical attraction was all good and fine, but unless it was one of the rare one-night stands he'd enjoyed when younger, Alex had reached the point where he liked to be friends with the women he took to bed.

Which is why last December, he'd been flabbergasted to finally realize a possible reason for *why* Yvette was so fascinating. Why, no matter how much they seemed to be two sticks of kindling irritating each other, he couldn't stay away.

Alex wasn't about to completely go off the deep end and say it was fate, but there were stranger things in the world. Heck, one of his best friends insisted that with his first wife, it had been love at first sight.

"I'll be right back." Yvette rose from the table suddenly.

Alex rose to his feet as she did, curious when she came back with a to-go container and began packing away the treats he'd bought.

She offered him a smile before leaning forward and lowering her voice slightly. "This place is going to get a whole lot busier over the next little while. I don't want to explain what we're doing until we're sure what we're doing."

"We're dating," he said firmly, but he was careful to keep his volume down.

"Yes, fine. But what we're doing *first* is going to my house where we will eat five million calories and open the day-one calendar thingy."

Alex took the container of treats from her, pressed the key chain back into her hand, then grabbed the sandwich bag. "I'll follow you to your house."

By the time he'd backed his truck up, she was waiting for him on the front porch of a of small cabin adjacent to the Heart Falls veterinary clinic.

At some point in the past, the building had started out as a dovetail-joined log shed. Over the years, the owners of the veterinary clinic had renovated and expanded until it was now a one-bedroom cabin heated by a wood-burning stove. Living there meant Yvette did the nighttime checks on the animals staying over at the clinic.

She looked at home standing at the top of the stairs, her well-faded Wranglers tucked into black cowboy boots that had been polished many times. The cold air had turned her pale cheeks red, and her dark hair stuck out from beneath the ear flaps on her woolen cap.

He supposed she had what people called a button nose. Yvette was cute and friendly. Most of the time she wore a smile, and everyone and anyone around her seemed content to spend time by her side.

He was such a sick bastard that what he liked the most, though, was when she got a flash of fire in her eyes. Her light-brown irises were beautiful, so light that there was a golden glow to them. Like spun amber or sunlight shining through the tips of wheat shafts. When she was mad, they all but snapped as if she had the power to light him on fire.

Yvette angry was a sight to behold.

But so was this. Curiosity was written all over her face as she joined him. He dropped the tailgate of the truck and climbed into the bed. He undid the straps holding his creation in place and slid the blanket-wrapped object forward until he could reach it from the ground.

"That's bigger than a bread box," Yvette said.

"It's a writing desk that's been in my family for a long time." Alex jumped down from the back of the truck. "Any ideas where you want me to put it?"

"This might be a problem." Yvette turned on her heel and headed inside.

He paused to grab their lunch bag and treats then followed her in the door. The place was warm, embers glowing behind the glass-fronted stove.

Beyond that, there wasn't a spare inch of wall space anywhere in the room. Yvette had bookcases and side tables and knickknack shelves everywhere. He'd known she liked trinkets, but this was spectacular.

Alex wanted to start at one end and work his way around, poking into every nook and cranny. Hopefully over this month, he'd get a chance to do a bit of that.

Right now he glanced toward the door at the end of the open room opposite the kitchen counter and table. "Bedroom?"

A snort escaped her. Her hand flew up to cover her mouth

as she lifted her laughing gaze to his. "Sorry. You're going a little fast for me there, Tiger."

It was his turn to snicker. "I mean, do you have more room in your bedroom?"

"Oh." Yvette shook her head. "Not really."

She shrugged her way out of her winter coat, revealing a long-sleeve shirt that clung to her sweet curves. Alex admitted to himself he was very much looking forward to getting to explore her bedroom.

Problem-solving first. Because if she wasn't opening his present, they weren't working on becoming friends. If they weren't becoming friends, they would never get to the becoming-a-couple part of this arrangement.

He dropped the food on the table then tilted his head toward the front door. "On the front porch works. It'll be protected from the weather, and it's probably better than putting it too close to the stove."

"I promise I won't burn it down," Yvette said.

He balanced the desk on his shoulder and brought it up the stairs a moment later. "I was thinking about some of the items I hid in here. They'll do better outside than near something hot."

"Oh, that's a hint." Yvette helped him manhandle the bureau into position behind the two Adirondack chairs she had faced west toward the mountains. "You have meltable things in the drawers. Which makes me think chocolate."

Alex unwrapped the thick wool blanket he had wrapped around to save the wood from wear and tear. "I guess you'll just have to wait and see."

He stepped back, checking immediately for Yvette's reaction.

He'd seen the writing desk a million times over the years before he'd begun work on it two weeks ago. In that short time, he—with his dad's help—had pretty much left the back and upper sections alone but replaced and installed a number of locks on the drawer fronts. It wasn't fancy, with no elaborate scrollwork or gold filigree. It was a solid working-man's household item that Alex hoped now held a bit of magic.

Yvette's eyes widened, and her mouth opened slightly. Her gaze dipped over the rows of small, square drawers on the top of either side then lingered on the far larger ones near the base. She stepped forward to run a finger over the top section in the middle that was covered by a curved, rolltop writing desk door.

"Alex. This is beautiful." She met his gaze. "The desk has obviously been around for a long time. Are you sure you want to give it to me?"

"Yes." If he had any doubts, the expression on her face would've wiped them away. She'd looked as if she'd won the lottery.

She stood silently before nodding firmly and turning with a smile. "Okay. No promises except to keep an open mind."

An alarm sounded from his watch.

Alex swore softly as he checked his messages before smiling sheepishly. "That's my warning. When I sent you the note, I didn't know what my work schedule would be. My shift at Silver Stone begins in half an hour. But I can wait while you open the first door."

"Oh. Right." Yvette pulled the key chain from her pocket and stepped toward the bureau. She paused then glanced over her shoulder. "Please tell me I don't have to randomly guess which drawer to open."

"Check your key," he suggested. "Then look at the drawers a little closer."

She glanced at her hand, turning the key chain over. Then she dropped to her heels, running her fingers over the front of the wooden drawers. "Oh, you're tricky."

She traced the outline of a Christmas tree on one of the smallest drawers, inserted the key in the lock, and opened it.

2

---

*T*he key turned easily, and Yvette pulled the drawer open to discover a slim envelope and another key chain. This new one was star shaped and shimmering gold, another small key dangling from the loop.

"It's very tempting to figure out right now which drawer this opens," Yvette told him, turning to Alex with the key in one hand and the envelope in the other.

"Now you see the fun part of having to wait a day. Anticipation." He waggled his brows.

"Irritation," she muttered, but amusement lingered as she slipped the envelope open. Inside was a gift certificate to Fallen Books, the local indie bookstore. The amount—

"*Whoa.*" She glanced up.

"Don't stop at the numbers, read all the way to the bottom," Alex encouraged.

A second later she spotted it. "...certificate is for *both* of us to purchase a selection of books to enjoy." That was sneaky. Only one problem. She eyed him suspiciously. "You're not going to try and pick out books for me, are you?"

"Definitely not. You get what you want. I'll get what I want."

His grin was back, although by the way he glanced at his watch, he had to be running out of time. "We can always trade later."

"Dude, life's too short to read bad books. And a bad book is one that's not up your alley."

"We'll figure something out," he assured her. "Consider it part of the adventure."

Yvette slipped the gift certificate back in the envelope, not quite sure what was supposed to happen next. "When do you want to go to the store?"

"Tonight works for me. I know they're open late. I can swing by and get you—"

"I'll meet you there," Yvette told him firmly. "Seven?"

Alex chuckled softly as he turned to go. "Okay. I'll see you there."

Damn, she wasn't letting him leave without any food. "Wait. Let me give you your lunch."

"Keep what you want," he insisted.

Yvette moved quickly, sliding a sandwich and a couple treats onto a plate for herself before wrapping up the rest and placing it in the bag.

She rejoined him on the porch and held the food forward. "Thanks. For everything."

When he paused only a step away, Yvette's breath caught in her throat.

He better not plan on trying—*anything*. Not today.

Only when he lifted a hand to brush his knuckles over her cheek, her feet froze in place. Her heart pounded, and her mouth was suddenly dry.

"See you tonight." Alex spoke softly, his deep voice stroking her senses. He tugged the bag from her white-knuckled grip then marched down the stairs to his truck.

She was still standing motionless on the porch when the red of his taillights vanished in the distance.

It took the cold breeze blowing across the wintry landscape

and tangling around her shoulders to snap her out of her partly hypnotized immobility.

Inside the cabin, she hastily ate lunch then headed back to the veterinary clinic.

A busy afternoon spent dealing with small-animal care offered her a wonderful distraction. She didn't have time for her thoughts to linger on the impossibly tangled situation she'd agreed to leap into with both feet. No one would possibly know that she was completely thrown for a loop by Alex and everything he'd started.

Or...maybe she wasn't doing as good of a job as she'd imagined.

Fingers snapped in front of her face. "Earth to Yvette."

She blinked, looking up to discover her boss's wife staring at her with concern. Lisa Ryder's dark-brown hair hung loose around her shoulders, her just-over-a-year-old daughter, Zoë, propped on her hip. Little Ollie, the family's cream-coloured terrier, sat at Lisa's feet, eyeing Yvette suspiciously, a soft grumble rising from her.

"Sorry." Yvette straightened, glancing around the waiting room to discover empty chairs. "Woolgathering. Ready for Ollie's checkup?"

Lisa nodded even as she pulled a face. "I asked for the last appointment of the day just in case." She shocked Yvette by passing over the little girl in her arms. "Here, you hold Zoë. I'll bring Ollie into the case room."

Zoë's eyes widened, but she patted Yvette's face as if giving the go-ahead. Lisa stooped to nab Ollie, and a moment later, they were all gathered in the examination room—Lisa holding Ollie on the table, Yvette holding Zoë.

The rumble of noise from Ollie continued.

"We need to do some juggling," Yvette said dryly. "Unless Zoë plans to do the exam for me."

"Right." Lisa made another face before taking Zoë and placing her on the chair at the side of the room. "You stay there for a minute, okay, sunshine? Mommy needs to help the puppy."

Yvette got her stethoscope out. She worked through the examination, still wondering exactly why Lisa seemed as distracted as she was. "Did Josiah say he was worried about Ollie? Because you seem nervous."

"Oh, that." Lisa patted Ollie absentmindedly. The pup wagged her tail enthusiastically and leaned into the caress, all the while managing to keep an eye on Yvette. "Umm, no. Josiah just likes for someone other than family to do her checkups."

"And...?" Yvette encouraged. No way was that all.

Lisa's cheeks turned bright pink. She glanced over her shoulder at Zoë, who was playing with the key chain Lisa had given her. She met Yvette's gaze and spoke quietly. "And the last time I was pregnant, Ollie got very protective, remember?"

"Oh my God." Yvette felt a smile stretch her face. "That's wonderful news."

Lisa held up a hand. "It's really early, so this is still hush-hush. But I'd already made the appointment for Ollie, and I didn't want to cancel."

Yvette focused her attention on the usually sweet little terrier. "Well, either she hasn't figured it out yet, or this time Ollie doesn't plan to be as protective, but I wish you the best of luck."

"Thanks." Lisa scooped up her daughter, pressing a kiss to her chubby little cheek. "This one is so much fun, we figured we'd better make another attempt before the brat genes rise to the surface."

"You mean before you end up with a kid just like you?" Yvette teased before adding reassuringly, "Zoë is adorable, the same as any kids you'll have."

"You're just saying that because my husband is your boss."

"I'm saying that because it's true. Also, I'm going to tell Josiah that when you have kids less than two years apart, Daddy gets to do night duty with the oldest one."

"Great idea," Lisa said. "Hey, I wanted to talk to you about Madison's baby shower. Can you come over tonight? Hanna is bringing Crissy, and my sister Tamara will be there with her brood, so we can chat while the kids play."

"Sounds fun." Normally she would've loved joining in. Spending time with the women she'd gotten to know in Heart Falls was a blast, but there was this other commitment she'd been obsessing over. "I'll have to take a rain check, though. I'm booked for tonight."

"Okay. What're you up to?"

Lisa was perpetually curious. There was absolutely no reason why Yvette couldn't answer that question honestly and easily. "Going to the bookstore."

Dammit. Her cheeks flamed. They had to be glowing red, especially considering the look Lisa gave her.

Yvette focused on Ollie, trying to ignore the question in Lisa's eyes.

Lisa fought back the worst way possible.

She stayed quiet.

"I'm meeting Alex." The words burst free, and Yvette sighed dramatically. "He gave me a Christmas calendar desk, and day one is books."

Zoë shook the keys enthusiastically, and Ollie barked, neither of which was enough to distract Lisa or kill the highly interested smile crossing her face. "*Really*? He gave you...a calendar *desk*?"

"Like one of those countdown-to-Christmas things. Only bigger." Awkward. She had to work on exactly what to call it. And what to call this thing going on between her and Alex.

"So, it's a date?" Lisa held up a finger. "Please, don't try to deny that, because you would not give up an evening with us to go to the bookstore."

"Maybe I just love books," Yvette said earnestly.

"Of course, you do, but you're still seeing him." Lisa reached over and patted her shoulder. "It's okay. I like him."

"It's only a date," Yvette said. Testing out the word felt... strange. "But I feel bad because I wanted to help plan the shower."

Lisa waved a hand. "It's not happening until early January. We'll chat a couple days from now. That will give me a chance to find out exactly how things are going between you and Alex. A full report."

"You're annoying," Yvette informed the other woman.

"So I've been told." Lisa grinned harder.

Finishing up with Ollie didn't take long. Lisa chatted easily about other matters, once again holding her little girl. Zoë laughed like a banshee as the puppy snuck in licks whenever possible.

The mood was light and happy, and Yvette floated out of the office with that contented sensation lingering in her veins.

She had a date. Alex was dating her. He'd made her a desk full of drawers filled with secret treasures, and tonight they were buying books.

It seemed magical. It seemed too good to be true.

It seemed too good to *last*.

Yvette shivered as the echo of thoughtless laughter rang in her memories. Her siblings, teasing. Taunting because she wasn't like them. Because her goals were different.

She was different.

Why can't you be more grounded, Yvette?

Jeez, kiddo, you need to keep both feet moving.

Silly girl, caught up chasing dreams. You're not good enough for him.

Not good enough for us.

Not good enough.

A cold wind blew over her as she approached the small house where she'd made her home for the past two years, making her shiver.

Anger shot in.

Screw this. Yvette shoved the gloomy thoughts away. She had a date. The voices could go stuff themselves.

FALLEN BOOKS SMELLED like adventure and hope.

Alex snickered at his poetic turn of thought even as he relaxed back into the easy chair he'd claimed, tucked into a comfortable back nook of the store. He closed his eyes and breathed deeply.

Crisp new pages, the faintest hint of scented candles, and some kind of spicy tea tickled his senses. Pretty much the perfect bookstore aroma.

They should bottle it or infuse it into a candle or something.

He'd arrived at six thirty so he'd have plenty of time to look around and make some choices before Yvette joined him.

Day one. Within the hour, they'd have officially started what Alex hoped would be an epic journey.

The part he had to get settled in his gut was to stop hoping for everything to go smoothly the entire time. It was hard, though. The more time he'd had to plan, and the more items that he'd put on his list, the easier it had been to imagine coming out the other end with Yvette by his side.

Damn optimistic soul that he had. He really needed to speak to his foster parents. Maybe he should have had fewer positive experiences during his teen years—that might've kicked the cheerful positivity out of his core.

They hadn't been perfect, but the one thing they had taught him was that success involved a lot of dreaming. Then it involved putting in the hard work.

So be it. The small moment of *keep it real* had just been kicked to the curb by one hundred percent holiday enthusiasm. Alex was going to do his damnedest to make sure when Christmas landed, he and Yvette were more than friends.

He flipped through one of his books, holiday carols playing in the background. Very appropriately, "I Know What I Want for Christmas" by George Strait came on, and Alex grinned as he hummed along.

"You understand this is a bookstore, not a library."

The statement was said dryly with just a hint of warning as Sonora Fallen settled into the armchair next to his. The woman was striking in a solid, contented way. In her early sixties, she had long, silver-white hair she usually wore in a braid as she worked the animal rescue at the ranch where she lived. Tonight she'd left her hair down, and for a moment Alex could see hints of what she would've looked like in her early twenties. Bold, fearless, and brilliantly beautiful.

Alex laid a hand on the pile of books on the table between them. "I plan to purchase them all."

"Huh." She leaned back in her chair and folded her hands in her lap then examined him closely. "You were gone for months."

"I was. I came back."

Her gaze remained fixed on his face. Assessing—which was a little worrisome, because she was not only smart as a whip, she'd been around a few times when he hadn't been at his best. Including one time when he'd managed to put both feet in his mouth regarding Yvette.

Sure enough, Sonora's brow rose. "While you were gone, did you learn any manners?"

Interesting to discover he was sitting upright, no longer slouched and relaxed but as if he were on inspection. "Yes, ma'am."

She made a sound that could possibly be called a snort before sliding his pile of books into her lap. Quietly, she examined each one before restacking it.

Alex had worked at the Silver Stone ranch for many years. Between that and his time at the fire hall, he'd gotten to know the foreman, Ashton Stewart, pretty well. Ashton, whom they were all convinced had a thing for the woman sitting next to him. Ashton was also in his sixties and usually said as little as possible about his relationship situation.

Which just made it all the more tempting for Alex to open the topic.

"I'll be seeing Ashton later," Alex informed Sonora.

Her hands remained steady as she turned pages. Her voice was cool as she answered, "I assumed you would."

Alex was about to offer to say hello from her when the bell over the door rang, and Yvette walked in.

He had closed the distance between them before she'd even reached the middle of the aisle. "You're early."

"I thought I would look around for a while," she said, lips twitching as she glanced at him. "You're earlier."

He grinned.

Sonora had disappeared, the curtain behind the desk still swaying. Alex would return to teasing her later if appropriate.

For now, he focused his attention on Yvette. "Have you been in before?"

"A number of times," she told him. She paused, and Alex smiled when he realized she was taking a deep inhale, appreciation drifting over her face. "I love that smell."

Alex gestured to the corner of the shop. "I've already got a few books picked out, so go ahead and look around. Want me to grab you a cup of tea?"

"Chai if they have it, please." Without a backward glance, Yvette drifted into the tall stacks with their colourful displays.

He turned to discover Sonora had reappeared, standing behind the counter with one brow raised. "The plot thickens," she murmured.

He cleared his throat. "Book lovers," he said in explanation.

"Ah." Sonora placed her hands on the counter and leaned forward. "Young man."

The temptation to stand at attention was strong. This woman must've been in the military in a past life. "Yes, ma'am?"

"That is a fine young woman." Her gaze barely flicked toward Yvette before settling on Alex, a very stern expression rising. "Behave."

"Ma'am, there is nothing you can tell me that my own mother hasn't already told me, multiple times, especially over the past six months," Alex assured her.

Which wasn't a *yes, I plan to behave* answer, because his list of what might happen over the next just-over-three weeks involved a fair bit of misbehaving. He hoped.

If all went well.

Sonora sighed. "You're as bad as my granddaughters. Don't think I didn't catch that little bit of doublespeak." She shook her head. "I'll get you the chai."

After that, Sonora seemed to have magically vanished. Perhaps, since she'd delivered her warning, she figured it was now on Yvette to take care of herself. Or maybe Sonora figured that while she poked and prodded Ashton as usual, she'd keep an eye on Alex at the same time.

Alex pushed all that aside and went after Yvette.

He found her in the true crime section. "Really?"

She already had three books in her stack. "Malachi Fields orders new mystery titles regularly for me. But this is a wonderful surprise."

She held up an oversized tome that involved serial killers and cold cases.

"Yvette Wright, are you telling me you like bloodthirsty books?"

"I like an eclectic mix of stories." She glanced to the side, where two steaming cups sat on the table between their chairs. "Let's see what you picked out."

A moment later she'd pushed her bloody books against his chest so she could settle in her chair and snoop through his pile.

Yvette turned over the topmost books and glanced up in surprise. "Fantasy. I never took you for a high-elvish type."

"Science fiction, science fantasy. High fantasy." He put her books on the side table, flipping the first one facedown so he didn't have to look at the cover with its image of blood dripping off a knife.

The glossy paint job made it look a little too real.

"Make believe," Yvette declared.

"Even the real stuff tends to have a bit of make believe in it." He leaned back and took the time to admire Yvette while she was busy reading the back-cover copy of his choices.

She'd pulled on a pair of leggings in a snowflake pattern. A blue sweater covered her curves, shadows accentuating her tempting form. Full breasts over a strong torso. Legs that went on for miles. Hands he wanted to feel stroking his chest the way she was running her fingers over the spine of the book—

Focus, dammit. Books, not ogling, were on the current agenda.

He forced his gaze to her face so that when he spoke, their eyes met. "I've read some history, but most of it is full of battles or people doing cruel things to others, and it's not my jam. Which is why fantasy history works better for me."

"A lot of history is nasty," she agreed. She sipped on her tea thoughtfully, her gaze drifting over him. "You don't have to buy me books."

What?

He must've said it out loud because she lowered her cup and leaned forward in her chair, expression concerned.

"I don't know if we should do this," Yvette said softly. "I mean, it's really sweet that you made that desk into something unique. You've obviously put a lot of effort into it. I don't want to knock that. But I'm just not sure this will work..."

"Because our reading choices clash?" Alex chuckled. He put a ton of energy into the sound, because if she called it off, they would be done. He would pursue her whole-heartedly, but only if she wanted to be pursued.

He wanted this to work. He *planned* on it working, but she had to feel in control.

Yvette eyed him in confusion. "Our reading choices don't just clash, they're night and day different. I will tell you right now, I have no interest in any of the books you want to buy."

"Trust me, I have no intention of reading yours." He shook his head and offered her a smile. "I'm really surprised, considering both of our jobs involve a fair amount of blood and grossness at times. I expected you to avoid it in your reading. But it is what it is."

Yvette watched him, waiting.

Alex rested his elbows on his knees. "Here's the important part. We both *read*."

Yvette's mouth was open, probably in preparation to once again tell him they needed to call this off before they'd even gotten started.

But now, she closed it. A small noise escaped her, sort of like a *humph*, and she dipped her head. "You're right."

"When do you read?" he asked, hope returning as Yvette settled. Thank goodness, she no longer looked about to bolt from the store.

"Whenever I can. Far too much." Yvette met his gaze. "I'm sorry. I'm a little skittish. I said I would trust you and give this a try. You've obviously not just put effort into this but a good deal of thought."

"No need to apologize. I get it," he assured her. "I'm on shaky ground here, as well."

For a moment they just looked at each other. The soft sound of Christmas carols chimed in the background as the warmth of the bookstore wrapped around them.

"When should I open the next drawer?" Yvette asked.

His heart kicked back into high gear. Good. They were still moving in the right direction. "Day two. Anytime you want tomorrow."

Her lips twisted slightly. "Let me rephrase the question. You said some drawers I'd open on my own, some with you. What's tomorrow?"

"On your own." He should have made it clearer in the first place. "I made a few assumptions, based on typical Heart Falls December activities. Did you plan to help pack holiday hampers for the food bank on Saturday?"

She popped open her phone and checked her calendar. "Yes. I'm off all day."

"Then, if it's okay with you, I'll bring lunch to your place. You can open day four, and we'll head to Rough Cut for the event at four o'clock."

"Are we planning on eating lunch the entire time? Because I don't know if I need that much pre-holiday consumption."

He laughed. "We won't eat the entire time. Your gift on Saturday is *some assembly required*."

Yvette nodded slowly before her eyes met his, and this time some of the hesitancy was gone. Curiosity and amusement sat in their place. "Okay."

Okay.

Day one. Plans made for day four. Alex pulled a book off

the shelf to his side, and for the next hour, they wandered through the store, talking about books.

The time together was a touch awkward by anyone's standard, but it was also far less antagonistic than some of their previous encounters.

It was a start, and that's all Alex could have asked for.

3

_____

*O*f course, the change in their relationship was now cannon fodder for discussion in the Heart Falls community. Alex discovered this the following day when he made his way into the fire hall.

His first shift now that he was back wasn't due to begin until two p.m., but the fire chief, Bradley Ford, had asked him to come in early. After Brad was good enough to let Alex take off at a moment's notice the previous year with no known return date, Alex figured there would be some payback for his good luck over the next months.

Not that he minded. None of the crew he worked with at the fire hall commanded anything less than his full admiration.

The two men Alex considered his best friends were Mack and Ryan. Mack Klassen, the head firefighter, was ex-military and as solid as they got. Ryan Zhao ran the local pub, Rough Cut, along with doing volunteer hours. Adding in Brad and Ashton, who also coordinated shifts at the fire hall, Alex was surrounded by a core group of men he knew not only had his back but were willing and able to kick his butt when necessary.

He raced up the stairs to the upper level, above where the

trucks were stored. The main area at the top was divided into three. First was the kitchen/gathering place where they served meals and met for technical training. The next section was the common room for quiet time and more relaxed conversations, with couches and easy chairs arranged in small groupings. The final area held the shower house and bunk rooms.

The one private room that had been previously occupied by Mack was still vacant. Over the past two years, Heart Falls had slowly increased their volunteer force until there were enough people willing to do overnight shifts, so they hadn't bothered to fill the space.

Alex hit the top of the landing and jerked to a stop.

As if thinking their names had summoned them, Alex glanced at the table in shock to discover not only Brad but the rest of the supervisory crew. Including Ashton, whom Alex had left not even twenty minutes ago at Silver Stone ranch.

Brad pulled out a chair and patted it somewhat ominously. "Alex, my man. Have a seat."

He hadn't expected running the gauntlet would be required, but Alex moved forward, striving to stay as outwardly relaxed as possible. "Well now, a twenty-one-gun salute. Nice you all took the time to come welcome me back."

Ryan grinned, black hair swinging across his forehead. As he leaned forward, mischief danced in his dark eyes. "This is the interrogation team. You need to pony up information."

"That's right, you do," Mack agreed. "Let's see, '*Hey, was just wondering. I need a little info and thought you might be able to help.*' Isn't that how all the emails started?"

"Mine did."

"Me too."

"Me three."

Shit. When he'd gone looking for information about Yvette, Alex had done his best to keep his questions on the down low.

He'd trusted that the guys wouldn't mention to each other what he'd been up to.

Looked as if he'd been wrong. Still, he wasn't going to confess to anything until he had to.

He dropped into the chair and deliberately slouched back, folding his arms over his chest. "Ask your questions, but I want it noted up front that the lot of you are worse than a proverbial group of gossiping old grannies."

"What else is there to do while we're sitting on shift from midnight till seven on a dead-quiet evening?" Brad asked. He rubbed his fingers over his beard. "Spill. What the hell are you doing with Yvette?"

"This isn't us being gossipy old women," Ryan hurried to clarify. "This is us keeping an eye out for a friend. Also, one of our ladies' good friends."

Alex snickered. "What you mean is that your wives are making you grill me."

"Sure. If that makes you feel better," Ryan said.

"I don't have a girlfriend, and I still want to know what's going on." This from Ashton.

Alex was so close to calling the older man on that fib. Everyone in town knew that Ashton and Sonora Fallen were *something*, even though they refused to come right out in public and admit it. But after his little conversation with Sonora the day before, Alex knew damn well the woman was curious as all get out. Which meant Ashton wanted dirt to be able to share with her, dollars to donuts.

Alex offered a nonchalant shrug. "It's like I told you when I contacted you. I wanted to make Yvette a gift, and I wanted it to be something she could enjoy."

"Good to see you're finally getting your act together and making a move. You're slower than molasses on a winter day." This from Ryan. His friend looked far too delighted.

Alex did his best Vulcan imitation. "Says the man who took

far too long to realize he was actually in love with his best friend."

"Yeah, but when he did finally clue in, he went double time at the whole leg-shackling and merging-her-into-the-family routine. Maddie looks ready to pop." Mack leaned forward and shook his head. "You're about to have a preteen and a baby in the same house. Glutton for punishment."

Ryan raised a hand in the air. "Madison's got experience with kids. And Talia is over the moon, although she's still a little worried it's going to be a boy. She thinks a little sister would cry less than one of the male persuasion."

"Not our fault that most of her friends had little brothers arrive," Brad said.

Alex snorted "Exactly whose fault do you think that is? I seem to remember you had a squawking son."

"Nice try getting us off topic." Mack leaned his elbows forward on the table and met Alex's gaze straight on. "So. You and Yvette."

"Hopefully, but there's no guarantees yet," Alex was quick to point out. "Look, I know this is partly because you have wives who are curious, and partly because you're all super snoopy all on your own. Here's the deal. You were all a big help putting together what I hope to be a great *get to know each other* scheme for December. I hope you'll see a lot of us together, but beyond that, back off and give us breathing room."

Ashton was grinning far too hard. "Don't know that we can do that."

Brad jerked a thumb in Ashton's direction. "What he said."

"It's not that we don't want to see you succeed," Mack explained. "It's just that shepherding you through this tricky relationship business is something we've been looking forward to for a long time."

"Bullshit." Ryan glanced at the other guys at the table before turning his own grin toward Alex. "They're all being far too nice. This is payback time, buddy. For all those times you meddled and all those times you pulled a fast one on us, we've got your back now."

"Why does that sound more like a threat than a promise?"

"He's damn smart. Some of the time," Brad said easily as he turned toward Ashton.

Ashton just chuckled.

Great. Not only was he going to have to manoeuvre Yvette into going along with his plans, he'd have to put up with well-meaning, interfering, brothers-in-arms as well.

So be it. "You're all a bunch of jerks."

"Definitely." Mack waggled his brows. "I hope you realize that no matter how hard you try, there's one thing you and Yvette will not succeed in doing."

Alex paused in the middle of rising from his chair. "What's that?"

Mack folded his arms over his chest and leaned back, amusement all over his face. "The now official Annual Firefighters' Ugly Sweater Contest. Brooke and I have got it all sewn up. Just you wait and see."

Laughter rang. Alex glanced around at the group of men before him. Combined with all the plans he'd made for this month with Yvette, something warm and happy eased through his entire system.

Good people. Good hopes for the future. He'd said it—nothing was guaranteed, but he did feel optimistic and determined.

He was going to make this the most memorable holiday season ever for one particular, beautiful veterinarian.

YVETTE HAD ALWAYS LOVED Christmas morning. She'd been one of those kids who could barely be convinced to go to sleep and was always downstairs staring at the tree far too early for anyone else in her family.

She adored that sense of anticipation and the butterflies it caused in her belly. It made her feel alive. Feel as if she was trembling on the verge of fantastic new discoveries.

The key she'd found in the day-one drawer had that same Christmas morning feeling to it. Lying in her bed, staring at the ceiling, Yvette timed her morning in order to prolong the giddy sensation as long as possible.

Alex had been right. Anticipation was a powerful drug.

She pulled the key ring out from under her pillow—yes, she'd been that obsessed. Leaving it somewhere by itself had seemed wrong.

Once again, the key itself held no secrets, but now that she'd had time to examine the star more closely, it was even shinier than first expected. When she clicked a small button on the back, the two halves slid apart far enough, she could clip the star onto something pointed, like the end of a pencil.

She needed to put these pretty trinkets somewhere she could appreciate them.

That idea was enough to get her legs moving, tossing back the sheets and sliding into the cool of the cabin. She took the time to get the fire going and put on the kettle before turning and assessing her options.

The one good point about how stuffed her living space was that she really could do anything she wanted. Unlike her mother and sister, whose pristine homes felt as if they'd taken the concept of minimalism to the point of monastery-like scarcity.

Might make them happy, but it was the furthest thing from comfortable and visually pleasing that Yvette could think of. She wasn't messy—which was usually the comment they made about her decorating style that got her back up the most. Having lots of things didn't mean there was dirt involved.

She had *treasures*.

"Okay. Refocus." Yvette deliberately covered her face with her hands and blew out a long breath.

This moment was to celebrate something fun and exciting, not to deal with family demons. Yvette stared at the star cupped in her hands and thought back to the previous night. To Alex and how it felt spending time with him.

There really was nothing wrong with what they were doing. Maybe nothing would come of this escapade, but she wasn't so overburdened with friends that she couldn't enjoy having one more.

Inspiration struck. Yvette reached under her table and pulled out a pad of construction paper. A few minutes with the scissors and a box of craft tacks, and she'd created a new masterpiece.

When she was done, the rustic country scene she'd picked up at a yard sale that summer had been repurposed. The canvas was covered with blue paper at the top, white at the bottom, with a very amateur Christmas tree nearly filling the rest of the frame.

Thumbtacks were pushed into the canvas, and the solid wooden backing in a random pattern would allow the pretty trinkets she found to be easily displayed.

Hanging up the first key chain—the Christmas tree—got bubbles percolating in her belly.

She deliberately put the star key chain on the table and made herself breakfast, taking care to watch her time. Fifteen minutes before she had to be ready for work, she found the drawer marked with a star and unlocked it.

Another key chain plus a small, cloth bag rested in the bottom of the small drawer. Yvette tipped the contents into her palm.

"Oh, Alex."

A silver charm bracelet lay in her hand, a tiny tree and a star already attached. A shiver stole over her skin.

She had wanted a charm bracelet forever.

Yvette hung both the star key chain and the candy-cane-shaped one for day three on her newly created Christmas tree wall hanging. She lined up the star so that it became a tree topper.

The charm bracelet she put carefully on the dresser in her bedroom.

Time sped past, with no opportunity to sit and pet the bracelet like she wanted to. Every instinct told her she should tell Alex it was too much.

She loved it, though. The bracelet was perfect. It was too much, and...

It was perfect.

She was pulling on her coat when her phone rang. Yvette answered without looking, gaze still locked on the pretty display in front of her and her thoughts still on Alex and this wild adventure he'd started them on. "Yes? What's up?"

On the other end of the line, an exasperated sigh rang out. "How do you expect people to take you seriously when you do such things?"

The happy bubbles in her system vanished. They didn't burst, they didn't fizzle out. They simply were wiped away by the sound of her mother's voice.

"Oh. Hi, Mom."

"Well, I suppose you don't usually answer the phone at that animal place of yours. But we taught you better than that. The first moment of a phone call sets the tone for what comes later, and in spite of your rustic career choices, you still need to be a professional if you ever want to succeed. I'm sure if you try, you can learn."

Maybe a hint of bubbles remained in Yvette's system, because the next thing out of her mouth was totally unexpected. "Did you have a reason to call, other than to lecture me?"

An instant snort of disapproval. "Yvette Elouise Wright. That was rude."

So was getting a lecture after simply answering the phone. Still, Yvette leveled out her tone. "I need to head to the clinic. Was there something you needed?" Sometimes redirecting her mother worked.

Sometimes.

"Your sister won another award. Top realtor of the month for November. Isn't that amazing? Carrie is far too modest to have told you, but we're all going out to dinner on Saturday to celebrate. You should join us. It would be wonderful to have the entire family together. You just don't come join us nearly often enough."

A twelve-hour drive, two directions, on winter roads, to have dinner with her family? "I can't get the time off right now, Mom."

As if she hadn't spoken, her mother continued, "Come Friday. You can see little Cassandra star in her school Christmas pageant. She is doing amazing, as usual. I'm so proud of those grandbabies of mine. I have to treasure every moment because they're growing up so fast, and I'll never have ones this little again to spoil."

Because at twenty-nine, Yvette could no longer have children? Blah. She debated *accidentally* hanging up but couldn't bring herself to make the final chop. "Like I said, I can't take time off right now. How are you and Dad?"

"Your father—he's amazing as usual, juggling all the volunteer tasks that he does. Simply unstoppable. He's probably involved with more things than you are, but then *he's* never been lazy. They asked him to oversee another event. Plus, he and I are co-chairs for the community fall fair."

Yvette ignored the passive aggressive criticisms and glanced at her watch, gauging how long she had before she could cut things short. "Sounds exciting."

"We've never done it before, but I told your father I was sure you'd be willing to help. You should know something about small towns these days. We would want that quaint, old-fashioned feeling. Right up your alley."

Gee, Mom, way to compliment and insult a girl all at one time. Which seemed to be a family specialty. Yvette nabbed the cinnamon bun she'd intended to save for later.

After most familial conversations, she needed a big dose of sugar and carbs to level out.

"We'll see." It was better to not make any promises. "Thanks for calling, but I really need to go. Bye."

"Carrie was also—"

Guilt shot through Yvette as the line disconnected in the middle of her mother's sentence. But the truth was, if Yvette hadn't cut the call off, they would've still been on the phone.

Sighing, she headed to the main office. Family was often complicated. Hers was awkward, uncomfortable, and horrifying all at the same time.

She slipped into the office, delighted to discover the head veterinarian, Josiah, was there, loading up his medical kit. It was the first time she'd seen him since she'd found out the news from Lisa. "I hear you've decided to keep filling the rooms in that enormous house of yours. Congratulations."

His ready grin was there, but his cheeks flushed. "It's very early days, so we're not saying anything yet."

"Lisa told me. Plus, if you really want to keep this on the down low for a while, you need to make sure nobody comes around Ollie," Yvette warned.

"Good point." Josiah nodded, his proud and enthusiastic grin still in place. "Oh, by the way. One change to your schedule this afternoon. Before you head over to the colony, I need you to stop in at Reiner's. He said he's got a couple of animals that need checking, and it would be a good idea to go before the weather changes. His road is a mess after a storm, and we've got snow in the forecast."

Yvette groaned. She really liked that her boss didn't try and protect her and trusted her enough to deal with even the old-timers.

But Reiner?

Normally she'd have no problem, but after a dose of her mother, she wasn't sure she had the patience to deal with a cranky old man.

"Could you take that trip?" She regretted the words the instant they were out of her mouth.

"Nothing doing. I told Finn I'd be out at Red Boot ranch two days ago." Josiah slung the bags over his shoulder even as his feet headed toward the door. He paused, turning back and giving her an understanding nod. "You've got this. Really. Also, Reiner likes you."

"Right. He hates my guts," Yvette said with a laugh.

"Now you're just being dramatic."

Yvette made her best attempt at raising a single brow, but she was pretty sure her expression looked tortured instead. "I'm not saying no, but I am saying you're delusional. Creighton Reiner would like very much if not just the female population but most of the *human* population on earth vanished."

Josiah was marching out the door. "Good thing he's not in charge, then. We'll see you later. Stay safe."

"You too."

Her words echoed off the door as it closed behind her boss. She took a deep breath and allowed herself the luxury of letting it out with an audible sigh. But even as she got that admittedly dramatic bit of complaining out of the way, she packed together everything she might need for a visit to the old-timer.

Creighton was one of the clients no one really liked to deal with, which had turned him into a strange sort of challenge for Yvette. Completing a visit without losing her temper had become a personal mission. It was kind of fun to see Creighton grow grumpier and grumpier as he failed to get a rise out of her.

He was rude to Josiah, growly and belligerent to every one of their veterinary suggestions, and downright nasty to people in town when he came in on one of his infrequent shopping trips.

Every time Yvette had been called out to his place, he'd loomed over her, watching and assessing with an expression that suggested she'd recently rolled in a freshly manured field.

Good thing he liked her. She hated to think how he'd behave if he truly had it in for her.

She snickered as she headed for her truck.

4

The trip up the steep gravel road to the old man's property took long enough for Yvette to sing along with a half dozen renditions of Christmas carols done up country- and western-style. Singing with Dolly Parton about a "Hard Candy Christmas" kept her from daydreaming about Alex and the mixed-up, hopeful emotions he'd triggered with this thing they were doing.

Arriving at the small farm, Yvette forced herself to focus on the here and now. The place was like any of a dozen in the community. Creighton Reiner, a gentleman now in his early eighties, had been a bachelor his entire life. Whether that was part of the reason why he was cranky or if he was single because he was cranky, Yvette didn't want to guess.

But he'd definitely done the place up in a way that made him happy. No trace of a woman's touch anywhere.

According to Josiah, Creighton had tried his hand at raising just about everything. Over the years, he'd had cows, goats, sheep, and llamas. The first year Yvette had arrived, he'd attempted to raise ducks. It wasn't a bad idea except that he was trying to do it with birds he caught in the wild.

She parked beside his beat-up old Ford, grabbing her kit with the intention of heading into the yard to track him down.

Something caught her eye.

She twisted back to examine Creighton's truck a little closer. It wasn't her imagination. The truck looked a little worse for wear. The front bumper seemed to have come into contact with something large and solid. Something immovable enough to have caused a vertical crack on the driver side. Leaning in, Yvette cursed to discover the entire bumper was being held in place with chicken wire.

"Dammit, Creighton." she muttered.

Whether it was a lack of money or because he didn't give a hoot, the wonky bumper wasn't something she could let slide.

She wondered if she could get her friend Brooke to visit the farm on the sly. Hopefully the woman could use her mechanic and body repair skills to deal with the problem before the man got a fine for driving a noncompliant vehicle on the highway.

Not that he left the farm very often, but if he did and then killed himself or someone else, Yvette would feel terrible.

The old-timer wasn't visible right off the bat, but the farm dogs were out in full force, a pair of them running eagerly to greet her from the far side of the barn. A couple more were visible in the distance, too old or tired to join the race but still with eager faces turned toward her.

She stopped to pet the two younger collies bouncing at her heels. "Hey, guys. How's it going? Yes, you are all good boys." Yvette slipped each of them a treat before gesturing forward with a hand. "Where's the boss? Where's Creighton?"

As if they understood, they turned and headed across the yard, barking enthusiastically. She followed them toward the small barn. Or oversized shed—she could never decide which it was.

Creighton met her at the door only to offer a tight scowl. "This way. Hurry up."

Yvette moved to follow, resisting the urge to roll her eyes. Still, annoyance pushed her into murmuring, in a gravelly, low tone, far too softly for him to hear, "Nice to see you, Yvette. Thanks so much for coming up my hellish driveway. Always appreciate skilled people taking time out of their day to help me."

She snickered, amused enough that by the time she joined him to peer over the railing into a small pen, her good mood was restored and her smile real. "Who do we need to check today?"

Three pigs, two goats, and a very skinny dog later, her smile had probably faded. Only it wasn't the animals causing her concern, it was Creighton as he hobbled painfully, leading her from place to place, his semi-ancient dog, Tex, moving at his side as if wanting to help.

Yvette snuck glances as best she could, but the old-timer seemed to be trying to stay out of her way enough that she couldn't see much more than a very worn pair of boots, one of which was wrapped with duct tape around the arch.

She focused on the animals until she was done with the final patient.

"There's not much else we can do for Hunter," Yvette told Creighton as she brushed a hand over the oldest retriever's head.

He had a well-worn but tidy dog bed tucked to one side of the front porch, and he moved slowly to curl back up in it after she'd examined him, tail thumping lazily as they continued to look in his direction.

Tex came and touched noses with the other dog before returning to Creighton's side.

"There's nothing specifically wrong," Yvette continued. "He is a little underweight. You might want to try and feed him inside the house. Or somewhere separate from the rest of the dogs to make sure he's getting his fair share."

The old man *harumphed* but didn't say anything.

Before he could move off the front porch, Yvette spoke again. Quickly, before the moment passed. "Want me to look at your foot?"

Creighton glared at her. "I'm not a dog."

She glared right back. "You're not a cow or horse, either, but I should probably still take a look at your foot and let you know if you need to see a physician." Blood stained his boot above the duct tape, which said it had bled a lot more than a simple cut.

For one moment it seemed he would simply dismiss her, but the next, he gestured with his head into the cabin.

It was the first time she'd ever been in the place. After seeing the sparse, no-nonsense way he dealt with things in the barn and outbuildings, the interior was not what she'd expected. She barely kept her jaw off the floor as she followed him into the tidy and cozy space. Timber-built furniture was everywhere, the light pine wood contrasting beautifully with thick, dark-blue cushions. The main decorations were beautiful bits of stumps and interestingly shaped rocks. Like a museum of natural wonders.

Yvette stifled her curiosity and focused on the old man who had settled into a straight-backed chair at the small table and was easing off his work boot and sock.

He folded his arms over his chest and glared daggers. "There."

A slightly blood-stained piece of fabric was wrapped around his foot, tied in place with strips of rags. Yvette loosened it carefully before whistling at the sight of the wound. "Well, now. That's a very impressive slice. Let me guess. Axe?"

Another *harrumph*. "Four days ago. Hit a knot, veered off. Went straight through my damn boot."

She examined his injury carefully, ignoring the fact he was growling at her more than the dog had. Thankfully, she was able to offer some positive news. "It doesn't look as if there's any infection, but it's deep enough that you should have stitches."

"You sew me up, then. I ain't going to town."

With anyone else, Yvette would have refused. But considering how seldom the man ever went to town, if she didn't do it, chances were he'd ignore her advice. Without stitches, the chance of future infection went up.

She went to work immediately. Complete silence fell over them except for the rhythmic ticking from an antique cuckoo clock on the far wall. It was strangely comfortable.

Stitched and bandaged, Creighton pulled a clean sock on and jammed his foot back in his boot. "Enough of that. Now, scat. Had enough of you poking and prodding into my business."

"You're welcome," Yvette said primly as she rose to her feet, surprisingly amused at his rudeness. "Always so good to see you, Mr. Reiner."

It wasn't until she was driving home that she realized what had amused her the most. He'd been trying to be annoying and shove her away, yet the entire time it had been clear something was on his mind. Something that had allowed him to accept her offer of help.

The less-than-vehement gruffness wasn't what she had expected. She made a mental note to talk to Josiah and see what else he could suggest going forward. She also considered sneaky ways to get someone with medical training to casually drop in to double-check she hadn't missed something during her examination.

Her time with Creighton was the biggest distraction she faced that entire day and the next. Which gave her too much time to think about Alex. Think about what they were doing.

Impatience rode her like a wild pony.

Day three, she opened a small, narrow drawer at the very

bottom of the right side of the desk to reveal a bottle of wine, a package of spice mix, and a note.

For your next girls' night out. The back of this card is a recipe for sangria. I'm glad you've got good friends in your life.

Saturday lunch seemed to take forever to arrive. She distracted herself the best she could, including taking the longest shower ever, singing "Carol of the Bells" at the top of her lungs along with LeAnn Rimes.

She was sort of reading when a solid knock finally sounded. Yvette shot to her feet, book abandoned, heart pounding with anticipation. She opened the door to discover the cowboy who'd been haunting her dreams standing there in all his muscular glory.

He also had a small bundle of grey fur held easily in one big hand and a sheepish grin on his face.

She shook her head even as she stepped forward to take the kitten from him. "Alex. I'm glad you didn't stick this in one of the drawers of the cabinet, but you can't—"

"Whoa. Not a gift. I found it. It was slinking its way beneath your truck, and I didn't want it to get any ideas about curling up under there." He glanced to the side of the porch, and his amusement vanished, a crease forming between his brows. "What the hell?"

He stepped to the side and lifted a small basket in the air. It was an old-fashioned picnic type, with a hinged lid, and from the sounds escaping, the kitten in her hands was only one of her current problem.

"Seriously? Why on earth would someone drop a basket of kittens on my porch?" Yvette wrinkled her nose. "That was a rhetorical question."

Alex placed the basket on top of the bureau then slid open

the lid to reveal two more little meowing bundles. "I'm sure you get a fair share of rescues dropped off here."

"It's gotten better since Sonora started the animal rescue, but yeah. People assume veterinarians adopt all strays." Yvette sighed even as she lifted the kitten in her palm in the air and looked the little grey fuzzball in the eye. "Hey, sweetie. I guess we'll need to take care of you and your siblings."

"Let me take it." Alex scooped the kitten from out of her hand and placed it back in the basket, closing and latching the lid. As soon as they were in the dark, the little things quieted down. "We can drop them off at the rescue before we head over to the pub."

Yvette gestured him in the door. "I may as well give them a once-over before we leave. That'll save me from being called in to do it later." She waited until he put the basket on the table and turned toward her so she could meet his gaze full-on. "So. Let's start this again. Hi. How's your day going?"

He stepped farther into the room, closing the distance between them. "Better now," he said. His dark eyes flashed with mischief even as one side of his mouth twisted upward into a wry smile. "This is going to sound silly, but it's true. I missed you the past couple of days."

The bit of bubbling in her system was back. "I—"

Why was this so hard? Why was it so hard to admit that she'd been thinking exactly the same thing not even an hour earlier?

He either sensed her discomfort or she simply lucked out, because he winked then turned back to the door, giving her some much-needed breathing room. "Before I take off my boots, let me grab lunch."

Yvette cleared off the table, bringing out plates. By the time he'd spread out the feast, once again purchased at Buns and Roses, her mouth was watering. Soup, grilled sandwiches, and another set of cinnamon rolls still warm from the oven. "This looks amazing."

"And delicious. That's a country onion soup. Tansy said it was your favourite."

"It is." Another rush of pleasure broke over Yvette that he'd deliberately picked food she'd enjoy. She offered a mock pout. "Tansy refuses to share any of her recipes."

Alex took a deep, appreciative inhale, his eyes closing. "As long as she keeps cooking, I'll keep buying." He twisted toward Yvette and raised his can of pop in the air. "To supporting local businesses."

She laughed. "Hear, hear."

He lifted his sandwich. "Now tell me about your morning. What's happening in veterinarian land?"

As the conversation drifted easily for the next few minutes, Alex gave up all pretense of being calm, cool, and collected. He let his gaze roam as he pleased, taking in everything from the crisp cut of her blouse to the tendrils of hair escaping her ponytail, framing her face.

As she ate, the charms on her bracelet clinked together with a small bell-like sound, and he ended up smiling around his mouthful of sandwich.

She followed his gaze to her wrist before lifting her eyes to his. "It's such a pretty bracelet."

"It's not really everyday wear for you, is it?"

"No, but it's beautiful, and I absolutely adore it. Thank you."

"Huh." He sat back and grinned. "I was sure I'd have to arm wrestle you to convince you to keep it. Or that you were going to give me hell for spending too much—which I didn't. Spend too much, I mean."

Her nose wrinkled in the most adorable way. "If you'd

walked into the room thirty seconds after I opened it, you would've been right. But given enough time to think it through, if I'm going to trust you during this dating thing, then I need to trust you know what you can afford. And also to know that expensive baubles aren't always the way."

Which was one of the things he had written on his list. The notes he'd made after speaking with his parents at the start of the journey.

She won't want expensive gifts but thoughtful ones.

Instinctively, he patted his pocket before catching himself and meeting her gaze. "You're welcome. I had fun putting together things I thought you would like. A couple of them cost something, but some of them are recycled. We'll figure it out as we go along."

The smile she gave him was worth every penny he'd spent on the charm bracelet—definitely not one of the recycled items. Not according to the dent in his pocketbook.

Still worth it.

They finished their lunch. Alex shared about the swing they were putting up for the older children on the ranch to enjoy and how a flock of chickens had unexpectedly gotten in the way. Yvette told him about being out at the Hutterite colony the day before when a section of fencing around a pig pen had mysteriously vanished, letting the entire stock escape. Hijinks and mayhem.

He'd always known their jobs were relatable.

Yvette pushed back from the table with a groan. "I am so full."

He glanced in front of her and chuckled at her abandoned half sandwich and drink. "I see you managed to finish the cinnamon bun."

Her cheeks flushed and body tightened. "Yeah, well..."

He paused. *Shit.*

Leaning forward, Alex met her gaze. "Backing up, because

that was supposed to be a tease that made you smile, not one that made you uncomfortable. You'll notice I also finished *my* cinnamon bun."

She nodded briskly then straightened. "Sorry. Still sometimes feel like a ten-year-old being told I can't have dessert until I finish everything on my plate."

He reached across the table and caught hold of the hand closest to him. "What was that you said about life being too short to read bad books? I think the same thing applies to food. Life's too short to not enjoy dessert. If that means I only eat half my salad and veggies, so be it."

She twisted her palm upward until she could squeeze his fingers. "That's a good life mantra."

"I'm glad you approve." Time for distraction of a different kind. "Let's get this table cleaned up before you open day four. We're going to need some room to work."

Not even ten minutes later, Yvette pulled today's key chain off a picture hung on the wall, so eager, she headed into the cold without pulling on a coat.

Alex grabbed both of their jackets, laughing as he laid hers over her shoulders. "Excited much?"

"A little," she admitted as she folded her arms and glared at the desk. "I cannot figure out which lock this key goes with." She glanced at him. "There's no clue that I can see."

He held his hand out, palm up. She laid the key chain in it.

"What is it?" he prompted.

"A feather." When he shook his head, she frowned. "Come on. Don't try to tell the veterinarian that is not a feather."

"Yes, it is a feather, but it's *more* than a feather." She was concentrating so hard he could almost see smoke pouring from her ears. "You can figure this one out."

"Give me a clue?" She slipped her arms into her jacket, rubbing her bare hands together as the sharp cold surrounded them.

He was tempted to offer a trade. He'd warm up her hands in exchange for a clue. Hell, he'd warm up more than just her hands—

Stick to the plan, his conscience warned.

"If you had a homework assignment at Hogwarts, you would use...?"

Her eyes snapped wide, and she snatched back the key chain to examine it closer.

"It's a quill. For writing. Which means it should open the writing desk part."

Yvette twirled back toward the bureau and put the key to the lock. She all but shouted as the long rolling section reaching from side to side smoothly pushed upward to reveal a large box and eight more small, locked drawers.

"Oh, my goodness. Okay, that also explains why there were way too few drawers for this to last all the way until the twenty-fourth." Her smile in his direction was as bright as the star at the top of the Christmas tree. "This is so much fun."

He reached past her and picked up the box. "Good. Now it's time for that *some assembly required* part of the date."

Watching as she slipped the tape open and pushed back the box flaps was as good as opening a gift himself. In that moment it was absolutely clear that Yvette loved presents.

Her mouth opened in a circle, and she cooed in delight as she pulled out multiple balls of coloured yarn. The packages of LED lights got placed beside them with a little more confused of an expression.

But it was the package of tiny zip ties that made her pull to a stop and glance at him, suddenly concerned. "Should I be worried?"

Amusement bubbled up. "Keep digging in that box, woman."

At the very bottom, he had layered two cardigan sweaters. His and hers in sizing but identical in pattern. Big red barns on the back, a fence line that wrapped around the waistline. Puffy white clouds against a blue sky and snow on the ground. A perfect Alberta-ranch-in-December scene built out of yarn.

Yvette pressed her fingers to her lips. When she dropped her hands, it was to clap them. "We're making ugly sweaters, yes?"

"I prefer the word *gaudy*," Alex said seriously.

"This is going to be so much fun." Yvette scrambled back into the plastic bags she had tossed aside in her hurry to get down to the bottom. "Alex. Tell me those aren't hand puppets."

"They *were* hand puppets, but now they're going to go on our sweaters." The puppets Yvette was pulling out of their wrappers fit on a single finger. All sorts of farm animals, including chickens and goats.

Alex joined Yvette in pawing through the pile, triumphantly raising his prizes in the air once he found them.

"You found people as well?" Yvette reached for the one in his closest hand, which happened to be the little farmer. "He's adorable."

She stroked a finger over his little cowboy hat then grinned up at Alex.

"You're adorable," Alex said in response, unable to stop the words.

A sudden pause, and her cheeks pinkened again. Only this time it wasn't discomfort like at the end of the meal.

Oh, she was embarrassed, but it felt...right. Like a connection growing between them instead of a wall shooting up.

Yvette pulled her gaze from his, stealing away the farm woman figure. "So, do we sew these onto the sweaters?"

"It's whatever we want to do," Alex said. "As long as the end result is super special so that it's painstakingly clear that *our* sweaters are way better than anything Mack and Brooke can come up with."

Something suspiciously like a snort escaped Yvette. "Not that you're competitive or anything."

He reached for the LED lights, ripping them out of their protective packaging. "Not competitive at all. You've got that right."

Yvette slipped on the smaller cardigan, buttoning it up the front before holding her arms out to the side and turning slowly. "It fits."

Dear God, did it ever. Snug against her hips, the sweater dipped in at her waistline then flared outward over her breasts. Alex forced his gaze to continue to rise, but holy hell, did he want to simply sit and admire her assets for a little while. He'd known she was curvy, but the sheer impact at this moment —breathtaking.

Lust-inducing. His body shot into high gear like a wound-up Christmas top.

Unaware of his dilemma, Yvette grabbed two packages and held them toward him. "I've got an idea. What if we light everything up, but instead of sewing the puppets onto the sweaters, we attach them with Velcro?"

He forced his mind away from its current path and concentrated on her suggestion. "That would be a lot of fun. Only I don't have any Velcro."

Yvette gestured toward the side of the room. "Trust me. I have a little bit of absolutely everything you could possibly need."

He was pretty sure she had more than a little bit of everything he needed.

Stay on task. "Great. Let's get started."

Considering how volatile their relationship had been a couple years earlier, it was bizarre how smoothly their afternoon went, working together. Thankfully, the Velcro she found didn't involve sewing. The super-sticky glue allowed them to put small squares on the back of the puppet pieces and strategically all over the sweaters.

Then they got to the tricky part. Yvette pulled on her sweater and pushed the LEDs into his hands. "It'll be much easier for you to see where to weave these in and out of the fabric if I'm wearing it."

Weaving meant touching. Sliding his hands over her torso as he stood close enough to smell her skin. The apple scent of her hair. The tempting sounds of...everything.

Dear God. *Easier*?

She had no idea.

Alex swallowed hard. "Turn around."

His voice sounded as if he had been gargling with gravel, but she'd already pivoted her back toward him.

He focused on what he was doing, but his fingers shook as he gently laid the long strands over her shoulder and then went to work. Weaving the end of the thin filament along the edge of the barn was fine, except for the heat coming off her body toward him.

It was when he began working along the top rail of the fence, the one sliding around her waist and headed toward the front of her body—that's when his mouth went dry and his heart started beating hard enough that it echoed in his ears.

Yvette's cheerful chatter slowly faded away. Her breathing accelerated as his hands brushed her belly. The full curves of her breasts swam in his vision.

Dammit, he was striving to keep this from turning into a moment that went too far, too fast. His gaze lingered on her heartbeat fluttering at the base of her throat. Her tongue slipped over her lips, leaving the bottom one wet.

Her hand came down on his forearm. Fingers curling around and holding him in place. She spoke barely above a whisper. "Alex?"

According to his timeline, he was already pushing to get

things physical between them a whole lot faster than most men would try. He'd be foolish to push his luck too hard.

Alex was no fool.

He was about to take a step back when she shocked the hell out of him. She wrapped her arms around his shoulders and squeezed him tight. Bodies coming into contact, heat wrapping around them. Sweet, lush woman pushed against every inch of his body.

Holy hell in a handbasket.

5

*E*ven as she hugged him, Yvette's mind raced. The sexual tension rising between them had been so big, it felt as if she'd been about to be blown over. Breaking eye contact by giving him a hug had seemed the safest solution.

Now that she was up close and personal with every heated inch of his muscular torso, she realized she might've made a teeny miscalculation.

Still, only one way forward. She forced air between them and stepped back, jerking her eyes up to meet his gaze. "I know that we're—still feels odd to say this—*dating*, but no matter how much I want to... I mean, it's too quick. I mean, it's not that I'm not inter—oh, *damn*."

He laughed. The sound escaping him was big and hearty and full of nothing but happiness. "You know, I pretty much understood every word of what you just said."

"Good for you," Yvette drawled miserably, "because I'm sure it was sheer gobbledygook."

"No, it's all right," Alex insisted. "You know how sometimes you get a text message from somebody, and it's mostly gibberish, but you still understand exactly what they meant? So you text back and say something like 'it's okay, I speak typo'?"

Amusement slid in, chasing away her embarrassment. "Yeah?"

Alex caught her fingers in his. "I also speak *awkward*. Which means I think you were trying to say that you feel the physical attraction between us, but it's too early to do anything about it. But it feels wrong to not do *anything* about it at all."

Which was a little too astute.

She folded her arms over her chest and glared at him. "Did you hypnotize me or something? Because that was just spooky."

The corner of his lips twitched upward. "Because I interpreted your *awkward* correctly?"

She nodded. "Pretty much one hundred percent correct."

This time he was the one to move farther away, gesturing toward the table. "Let's redirect this a little. Not because I wouldn't love to continue down the road we just started, but I want us to enjoy the journey. We will not give in to any physical urges today, no matter how much we want to. Agreed?"

Yvette nodded mutely.

"Okay. Then how about you take off the sweater, and we'll finish up on the table?"

"Good idea." She wiggled out of the cardigan and pressed her hands to her cheeks in an attempt to cool them down. "Maybe I'll grab us both cold drinks."

He chuckled softly, but again his grin was one of a fellow conspirator, not judgmental. "Sounds like a plan."

Even with a little more room between them, Yvette was still intimately aware of his every movement. Every time their arms brushed together an electric shimmer raced over her skin.

Now the sensation was something delicious. Tempting, with no hidden agenda or worry that she would do something wrong.

She was comfortable around this man she barely knew in

many ways, and that was enough to fill her mind and make her consider all sorts of questions she could ask. All sorts of things she wanted to know.

In the meantime, they worked on the sweaters.

Once they were done, the gaudy creations were put away for the following week and their big reveal at the annual firefighters' holiday gathering. Yvette took Alex over to the clinic and got him to help her check out the kittens and give them their first shots.

The sky was turning to twilight when he guided her toward his truck and placed the basket of kittens in her lap. "We'll stop at the shelter before heading to Rough Cut."

"It's good to have the shelter around," Yvette shared as they headed down the highway. "It's always better when sweet little creatures like these can end up in a happy home."

"I always get a kick out of the cats that live around Silver Stone," Alex admitted.

"Having them there is part of a healthy ranch. They're work animals, same as horses and dogs." Yvette peeked into the basket, a small black nose poking out at her. "So sweet."

"You don't have any pets." Alex glanced sideways at her.

"You don't either," she snapped before interrupting herself with a raised hand. Jeez, could she be any more uptight? She lowered her voice to a normal tone. "And... Let me try that again. It's true. I don't have any pets right now, but that's more about where I live and the job I'm doing than me not wanting to have one."

He reached across the distance between them and caught hold of her hand. His calloused fingers brushed her knuckles, his thumb sliding over the back of her wrist. "I won't break if you talk to me in something other than a well-regulated tone. But thanks for starting that over. I wasn't making a judgment."

Which is what Yvette had realized only seconds after reacting. She glanced at their joined fingers, adjusting until the positioning felt both comfortable and fraught with danger. "I know you weren't. *You* haven't done anything wrong."

"Oh, don't worry. Give me enough time, and I'm sure I can pull off something foolhardy."

Yvette sat quietly before confessing the truth. "I'd like a pet, but until I know I can care for it and give it enough attention, I get my animal-loving quota from work. I've seen too many times when well-meaning people get pets then semi-mistreat them by not being available." She glanced up and met his eyes briefly. "I don't want to be that person."

He squeezed her fingers and added a quiet, "Good for you."

They fell into silence. Yvette was a little embarrassed at her confession but also proud that she'd voiced it. Sitting together was once again more comfortable than awkward.

They were still holding hands when they pulled into the yard at the animal shelter. Sonora Fallen's house sat to the south of the spacious old barn that had been renovated a couple years earlier into its new purpose.

Alex chuckled. This time his amusement held a hint of a naughty tone. "Well, well, well."

Yvette followed his gaze but couldn't see what was so entertaining. The only thing out of the ordinary was the tail end of a truck sticking out on the far side of the house. "What's —? Oh. Oh, *really*."

That was Ashton Stewart's vehicle, mostly tucked out of sight.

Yvette twisted toward Alex and offered a grin.

He waggled his brows. "We *have* to drop off these kittens. I do hope we're not interrupting anything."

She waited until he came and opened her door, looking around the entire time for any signs of activity. Nothing, and when they checked it, the door to the animal shelter was securely locked.

Yvette turned and led Alex up to the front steps of Sonora's house. "I really should feel terrible about this," Yvette confessed.

"Me too. Strange, though. I don't. Just curious and wickedly amused." Alex put his knuckles to the door and rapped loud enough that there was no way anyone could pretend to not have heard the summons.

"Just a minute," Sonora called.

Yvette leaned against Alex's side. "You think she's hiding him in a closet?"

He was still chuckling when the door opened and Sonora came into view. Her long, grey-white hair was up in a messy bun, her cheeks glowing and her eyes bright. "Yvette. Alex. Hi."

"Hi." It was tempting to continue to tease, but at the same time, Yvette felt a little pity for the woman. "The shelter's locked up, and I found some abandoned kittens."

"Oh. Of course. Come in." Sonora stepped aside and gestured them forward. "It'll just take me a minute to get my things."

"We can stay out here," Yvette offered.

"Definitely not. Come in out of the cold. I insist." Sonora all but attacked Alex, grabbing hold of his arm and jerking him into the house so she could shut the door firmly behind him. "Stay here."

She whirled on the spot, heading to the side wall where winter boots and coats waited.

Alex's eyes twinkled so hard, Yvette wanted to elbow him in the side and tell him to behave.

"How's your day going?" he asked Sonora oh-so-innocently.

"Fine. Just being lazy."

Yvette bit her lips together to keep from saying something as she spotted a familiar truck quietly rolling past the living room window.

Ashton, stealing down the road and away from his secret tryst.

Once Sonora led them outside and into the shelter, things went quickly enough. It was probably less than ten minutes before Alex and Yvette were back on the road, heading in silence toward the charity event.

A silence that lasted only seconds before Alex outright snickered. Which made Yvette choke on a snort that escaped. They weren't even at the main highway before Alex pulled over because he was laughing too hard.

Yvette gasped for air. "You saw Ashton sneaking away?"

"A blind man would've spotted him. The man is part ostrich. Pretending you're invisible doesn't make you invisible."

"You going to tell him that?" Yvette asked.

"Why spoil his delusions?" Alex wiped tears from his eyes.

"Did you see Sonora's blouse?"

He coughed then met Yvette's gaze. "Um. Do I want to know?"

The older woman had been perfectly decent, but Yvette had noticed her buttons had obviously been fastened in far too much of a hurry. They were completely out of line. "No. I guess not."

They smiled all the way over to Rough Cut.

Upon opening the door for Yvette, Alex marched into the familiar pub on her heels. Rough Cut was a laid-back dance floor and watering hole during most of the week, but as her owner, Ryan had been trying to make it into a community gathering place as well. Over the past year, with Madison by his side, more than drinking and adult socialization happened at the place.

This annual event was one that made Alex happy to join in and offer a hand. Putting together food boxes for families in the community who needed a little extra help was always a good idea but especially at this time of year. Alex knew that far too well from his early years with a mom who always had less money than they needed each month.

Ryan waved him over, pushing his dark hair back out of his eyes before grabbing a box of supplies. "The truck showed up late, so we're running behind. Can you help me stack these beside the sorting tables?"

"Give me your coat," Yvette said, tugging on Alex's sleeve. "I'll send over some more muscle as soon as I can. Okay, Ryan?"

He nodded. "Madison was tracking people down as well. Can you do me a favour, though, and sit on her? If she tries to lift anything bigger than a cup of hot chocolate, let me know."

"I can give her hell all on my own," Yvette assured him. She glanced at Alex and wiggled her fingers. "Catch you later."

"Count on it."

It took longer to set up than usual, what with boxes to haul across the dance floor. But even as the supplies were gathered, Ryan's assistant manager, Grace, got the assembly line up and running. Filled boxes were transferred to vehicles for delivery that evening.

In fact, by the time six o'clock rolled around, they'd accomplished everything they needed to before the pub doors opened and the public began rolling in.

Grace returned to her spot behind the bar, while a small group of volunteers remained settled around the table they'd claimed for their own. Brad and Hanna. Ryan and Madison. Brooke and Mack.

Yvette and Alex. It felt good to be thinking of them as a couple.

Alex shifted his chair until he was right up next to Yvette. Wrapping an arm around her shoulder casually but very clearly claiming territory as more of the locals filtered into the bar.

Gazes lingered on them, a whole lot of cowboys stopping to take note of his presence at her side.

Yup. More than one man in Heart Falls would've been willing to take the sweet veterinarian dancing—and they could interpret that anyway they wanted to—but Alex intended to be the last and only man holding her in his arms.

"Is it just me, or was that more tiring than last year?" Madison leaned her head against Ryan's shoulders. Eyes closed.

Brooke laughed. "Maybe it's the bowling ball under your shirt that made it a little more exhausting."

"Watermelon," Madison corrected. "Bowling ball does not come close to describing the dimensions accurately."

Mack leaned forward, palms pressed to the table as if about to share a secret. "Just don't suggest anything bigger. You know, like a whale or a Goodyear blimp. I have it on good authority that homicide charges don't stick if the perpetrator is eleven months pregnant."

Madison barely moved except to roll her eyes. "You're lucky you're over there, and I'm over here. Because that deserved a punch in the arm."

Instantly, a loud *ouch* escaped Mack's lips, and he pivoted his head to scowl at Yvette, who sat beside him. "Hey."

She blinked innocently. "What? I swear I didn't do anything. It must be those mischievous holiday spirits, secretly granting wishes."

Alex gathered her closer, holding a warning hand toward Mack. "Don't even think about retaliating."

"You're no fun," Mack complained before winking at Yvette. "Trust me. I'll get my revenge later."

"Yeah, he plans to step on your feet while you're dancing," Brooke warned.

Mack straightened suddenly, shooting to his feet. "What a brilliant idea. Yvette, dance with me."

"Oh. But..." She paused then nodded, even as she eyed Brooke. "I guess."

Brooke waved a hand. "Go. Wear him out a little first, there's a sweetie."

A moment later Alex watched his date dance away with one of his best friends.

"That was a twist I did not see coming." He turned back to the table and shuffled his chair closer to Brooke's. "What're you up to?" he asked softly.

Because this had to have something to do with the guys' threat to be interfering busybodies.

Brooke took pity on him. She grabbed him by the hand and hauled him onto the dance floor as well, whirling them in a rapid two-step as she spoke. "Yvette is a wonderful, fantastic woman."

"Agreed." Alex adjusted his grip on Brooke to hang on a little more firmly so he could retake control and start leading. "What does that have to do with your husband stealing her out from under my nose?"

"I told him I wanted to talk to you. He's good like that. Especially when I offer outright hints." She offered Alex a big grin before turning thoughtful. "I like you. I've heard good things about you over the years, and I've enjoyed *most* of the time I've spent with you, but I'm still giving you a warning. You need to take this thing you're doing with Yvette seriously."

Which was exactly what he planned. Still, Alex was more curious than angry at that point. "Rather than ask you what the hell you think I'm doing, I'll let you keep explaining."

Brooke made a face. Her next words came out in a bit of a rush, as if she were saying it before she could think better of her decision. "I won't spill her secrets, but at the same time, she's got triggers. She's got the biggest heart of anyone I know, which means she takes people at their word. If you tell her one thing and then change your mind, it's going to really hurt."

Which was another thing he had on his list. *Generous heart, soft heart.* "I got that. I'm not pissed off at the reminder."

"But you tease. And that's not always going to go over well. Not because you mean to be an asshole but..." Another pause. Brooke shook her head. "Just give her some grace, okay? If she seems to overreact?"

A touch of understanding slipped in. Little moments, like her too-quick reaction to his innocent comment about not having a pet. Being overly worried that what they were attempting wasn't a good idea.

Triggers. Why she had them was a separate issue, but knowing they were there was good.

Alex nodded at Brooke, refusing to ask for more information. The warning had been enough, and now it would be up to Yvette to explain when she was ready. "I can do that."

"Good. Because if you hurt her, we will make your life a living hell." Brooke somehow managed to bat her lashes and keep time in the dance.

"Duly noted." Alex grinned. "Thanks for the recommendations for her gifts, by the way. Your advice is going to be the biggest hit of the whole calendar."

Brooke pulled on an innocent expression. "I don't know what you're talking about."

"Oh, come on. I might have asked Mack for advice, but I knew damn well that anything I asked him, he would turn around and tell you about. Which means the tidbit about Yvette wanting a charm bracelet was your idea." Alex twirled her hard, setting a path to intercept Yvette and Mack. "So, thanks. You're brilliant."

She grumbled a little. "Fine. You're welcome."

The music changed just as they twirled to a stop beside Mack and Yvette. Alex was reaching for her hand when another couple swung between them.

"Come on, Yvette. I need to ask you something." Brad Ford

gently pushed his wife toward Alex. "Try to keep him out of trouble, Hanna. No running into anyone."

Ten seconds later Alex was dancing...but not with his date.

The petite brunette in his arms laughed softly. "You should see your face right now."

Alex glanced over Hanna's shoulder to spot Brad whirl Yvette across the floor away from them. "I'm being managed. That much is clear." He glanced down at her. "Hey, Hanna. Long time no see. How are you, darling?"

"I'm good. My children are healthy and happy, my husband is a joy, and my friend is dating someone who makes her hopeful." Hanna's smile bloomed even brighter. "The way you reacted to that comment makes me even more optimistic."

"I'm an optimistic-making kinda guy," Alex insisted even as his amusement rose higher. He figured his friends would be pains, but their wives all leaping in as well...

Sudden inspiration struck. What a perfect opportunity.

"Why do you now look as if you've got mischief on your mind?" Hanna shook a hand free so she could poke him in the chest. "Spill the beans."

"What happened to the quiet, innocent woman who married my friend? You've gotten awfully pushy."

Pride rose in Hanna's eyes. "This is what a woman looks like when she knows she's unconditionally loved."

"I'm so damn glad for you both." Alex leaned a little closer. "I need a favour."

It took a few minutes to explain, but when he was done, Hanna was both rolling her eyes at him and laughing. Alex took that as a good sign.

When they rejoined the others at the table where Madison and Ryan were waiting, Hanna caught Alex by the shirt front and tugged him toward her.

"You have potential. Don't mess this up," she whispered before planting a kiss on his cheek.

Brad guffawed even as he hauled Hanna into his arms and mock glared at Alex. "I said you could *dance* with her."

"Hey, *she* kissed me," Alex protested, sliding his arm around Yvette and tugging her toward the dance floor. "Now before anyone else can interrupt us, excuse us."

Yvette settled against him, her body a little stiff. Thankfully, the music changed, and the beat slowed. The crooning ballad in the background about starry nights and sweet kisses allowed Alex to slowly close the distance between them until her soft curves were tight against him.

"That's better." Alex rested his cheek to hers. "Hey, sweetheart. Took a while to get here."

"I feel as if I just went through some kind of gauntlet." Yvette peeked back at the table full of their friends then met Alex's gaze. "Did my friends all threaten you with bodily harm?"

"Not *all*," Alex rejoined. "A bunch of them aren't here, and Madison didn't get a chance yet."

A soft groan escaped Yvette. "Sorry."

"Please tell me that you weren't being warned off spending time with me by the guys."

"Oh, no. Definitely not." Yvette snickered.

Alex pulled her closer and made a tight turn, because holding her in his arms was so good. "Don't stop now."

She smiled into his eyes. "I've had all your charms expounded to me, in triplicate. Ryan got in a few comments at the table before you got back."

"Fantastic." Alex wondered where the nearest wall was, so he could bang his head into it a few times. "Now you're going to run as far and fast as possible."

"Or maybe not." Her expression grew a little more serious. "You told me you were doing this for some reasons that were a little far-fetched but also very sweet."

"I like sweet," he said quickly. "I can work with you calling it *sweet*."

She stared into his eyes. "Alex?"

"Yes?"

Yvette hesitated then lifted her chin. "Kiss me?"

6

His grip on her body tightened for the barest second. "Kiss you?"

"I was thinking about *awkward* messages. Speaking them. Which I'm very good at, by the way." Yvette was screwing this up in so many ways, but at the same time, to hell with it.

The entire day until now had been leading to this. Their time making a silly craft. The connection in finding secrets regarding Sonora and Ashton. Even packing the food hampers and the time dancing with all his friends. They'd all coalesced into a whole that said Alex Thorne was trying his damnedest to be a man she should take seriously.

Her libido agreed with that message, loud and clear.

So, time to step forward boldly, even if it seemed quick.

She brushed her fingers against the back of his neck in a gentle caress. Her gaze slipped from his eyes to his lips before she could stop herself. The words came out soft and husky. "It was right to stop earlier, but what I really, truly want right now is a kiss."

A ballad was still playing, so him rocking her slowly against his body didn't look one bit out of place.

The wicked chuckle that teased her hearing, though? That was pure sinful pleasure. "You set the speed, sweetheart. But just to make sure you know, I'm fully on board with your request."

He pressed his big palm against her cheek, thumb extending to one side to cradle her chin, then he leaned in and their lips met.

It started as a soft brush that instantly went harder. Alex angled her head to the side more so he could take control of her mouth. He stroked his tongue insistently over her lips until she opened, and then—*dear, God*—it was good. The man kissed hard yet with a controlled power that said this wasn't yet the extent of what she could expect.

His free hand fell to her lower back, pressure increasing until there wasn't a lick of air between them. She'd thought the connection was close before, but now every ridge of his abdomen teased her body and made her long for skin-on-skin contact. The thick length of his erection was right there, plain as day. Solid as...

A sharp nip on her bottom lip stole a gasp from her and broke off her mental ramblings. "Kiss me," he ordered.

God, she was getting light-headed, but what a way to go. She slid her tongue against his, a chill zipping over her skin as a sexy groan rumbled up from his chest.

She felt it all the way down to her toes.

He broke apart from her slightly. His lips curled upward, still connected to hers.

"What's so funny?" she whispered.

Alex rocked her to the side, his lips moving away from where he'd been thoroughly stealing her senses. Thank goodness, because she'd been a second away from swooning or something equally ridiculous.

His mouth teased along her cheek and landed under her

ear—and maybe she wasn't done with the being-overwhelmed bit.

His whisper was full of amusement. "Kissing you for the first time on the dance floor? Pretty great, in spite of a multitude of chaperones and on-lookers, every one of them hoping we go on for a moment too long so they can shout rude suggestions."

Oops. She jerked back to see who was—

Or at least she tried to jerk away. It was like trying to move a mountain,

She stayed stuck against him, up close and personal. His grip remained firm, and he laughed again, deep and dirty. "Uh-uh. No use running, since we've already got the audience."

Yvette took a deep breath and recalibrated. That sensation running up her spine was less embarrassment and more...

Pride?

Well, damn. She rocked another couple times in his arms as she considered that revelation.

A very sexy and attentive man had made it clear he not only wanted to spend time with her but had kissed her right out in public. It had been a great kiss, and she was looking forward to another.

She deserved this attention, and moreover, since he'd said all along that he was angling to be with her for kisses and more, she could enjoy this attention without guilt or fear.

"Maybe we'll have a series of first kisses. All sorts of locations, that sort of thing." She met his gaze then winked. "We can rate them."

He twirled her hard, laughter spilling free. "I look forward to that, Ms. Wright. Every damn one."

The evening continued with plenty of laughter, dancing, and time with good friends.

Turns out Yvette got her second *first kiss* at the door to her cabin when he dropped her off. This one was slow and steamy, and when he pulled away, his dark eyes glittered in the moonlight. "That was also a pretty good kiss. Eight out of ten?"

"Sure." The word came out a little shaky, but Yvette smiled, fingers tangling around his as he stood close enough to warm her. "Thanks for a great day."

"I love spending time with you," he said softly. "Enjoy your days five to seven, and I'll see you on Wednesday."

"Wait." They had both talked about being busy and that she could open the next few days on her own. But with how well this day had gone, Yvette didn't want the magic to end. "You're welcome to drop in if you want to be here. I can hold off until you have the time to join me."

He stepped closer, hands settling on her hips. "That invitation makes me feel very happy. And then stinking mad because I can't take you up on it. Not yet."

Like a splash of cold water, her happiness shriveled. She moved quickly to respond in a way that made it clear she didn't really have any sort of agenda. "It's okay. I just thought maybe it would work. Don't worry about it—"

His fingers tightened briefly, grip firm. "Sweetheart, you need to shut up for a minute before I decide you need a spanking for jumping to conclusions too damn fast."

Okay. Yvette's emotions were on a yo-yo string. Hopeful, then annoyed at herself, and now annoyed at him. She folded her arms over her chest. "Did you just threaten to spank me?"

"Not a threat if it's something you want, but hush." He pulled her in and lifted her chin so their faces were only inches apart. "I'm getting sent down to Pincher Creek for the next three days. I *can't* come over, but if you want to call or text, I'm as close as technology can make us."

A rush of heat flooded her cheeks. If only a hole would've opened up underneath her so she could've vanished, but no. She was stuck right there with his intent gaze fixed on hers. She spoke softly. "I did jump to conclusions again, didn't I?"

His grip on her chin relaxed, his finger brushing easily over her cheek. "It's okay, as long as you don't mind me bouncing you back to the way we need to go."

She nodded slowly. "I'm good with that." She met his gaze and tried a cautious smile. "If I kiss you now, is that considered our first make-up kiss?"

"Damn if I care what you call it if the result is that I get your lips on mine."

Then he was holding her, and they were kissing again, and Yvette was once again wondering what kind of fairy tale she'd stepped into.

After, she stood beside the calendar bureau, the solid wood under her fingertips as she watched his truck vanish into the distance.

Sunday was the day Yvette visited with her grandparents. The main reason she'd moved to Heart Falls two years ago was to get to know Floyd and Geraldine Wright better. After spending time with the older couple, she was pretty certain now that their family's odd estrangement was more her parents' fault than her kindly grandma and grandpa's.

She joined them in the common room, stopping beside her grandma and examining her with concern. "Grandma? What's wrong?"

Her grandma sighed. "Getting older is rough. That's all, sweetie."

Grandpa Floyd was staring out the window, a happy smile on his face as he watched the birds flitting to and from the feeder that was well stocked with sunflower seeds.

Yvette stooped beside his wheelchair and pressed a kiss to his cheek. "Hello, Grandpa. I've come for a visit."

He smiled at her. "Well, isn't that nice." He caught hold of her hand and patted it gently. His age-worn hands frail and soft like a butterfly's kiss. "Vilket härligt leende."

Yvette glanced at her grandma. "What's that mean?"

A sad smile crossed her lips. "He said you have a beautiful smile. Come. Sit and visit for a while."

Grandpa Floyd was once again focused on life outside the window, so Yvette moved closer and settled at the table. She filled a cup with tea and topped up her grandma's when the woman nodded at her question.

Comfortable silence fell for a minute while they took their first sips.

Then Grandma put her cup down and placed her hands on the table. "Your grandpa needs to move into the other section of the home soon. Where it's a little safer for him. He's getting forgetful, you know."

Yvette laid her hand over her grandma's and squeezed gently. "I'm sorry."

"Oh, I am too. But I'm also glad that we're here, where I will only have to walk down the hall to see him every day." Brightness shone in her grandma's eyes, moisture that she dabbed away before straightening and putting on her happy face. "We're both healthy, as much as we can be. We have a lot to be thankful for."

"Do you need help moving him?" Yvette asked.

Her grandma nodded. "That would be nice. It won't happen for a week or so. It's not about moving furniture or anything like that, but it would be good to have you there when we settle him. Even though he forgets a lot, he loves to have you around."

"I'm happy to be able to help," Yvette said honestly. "Just let me know when, and I'll make it happen."

Grandma Geraldine smiled. "That's another blessing. Having you in our lives. So many years that we didn't have, but I will always be thankful for the time we have enjoyed."

Maybe it was the emotion inside, churning from the moments she'd gone off the rails with Alex. Yvette was smart enough to know where the root of those discomforts came from.

She'd learned lessons from her family that were not positive.

Still, she was a little shocked when the words escaped. "Do you ever wish you were still in touch with my mom and dad?"

"Oh, sweetie." Grandma shook her head slightly. "Rarely does a mother *want* to be separated from her children. But I can be sad and yet smart enough to understand there's nothing I could have done to make things better. Not without compromising what I know is right."

Which made sense on so many levels. "You're braver than I am," Yvette confessed softly. It wasn't a full-out statement wishing that she could also break all ties with her family, but it was as close as she could get right then.

"My dear." Her grandma held her arms open and waited until Yvette slid in close enough to accept the tight embrace. "You are still working through who you are and what's important to you. The journey takes time. Never apologize for that."

In his seat by the window, Grandpa Floyd began singing. A song Yvette remembered from her early years of growing up before her family changed. After giving her grandma a final squeeze, Yvette pulled her chair beside his so she could join in with the harmony.

His gaze darted to her face, and while the sweet song rang on the air, his voice trembling slightly, he smiled.

Yvette might still be on a journey, but moments like this were bright and shiny and gave her hope. Filled her with joy.

The desire to tell Alex everything grew bigger. To share the bits of the past that were getting in her way and to brainstorm ideas for the future. To see what the man with the laughing eyes would suggest while they travelled this path he'd set them on.

Alex: Is it snowing as hard in Heart Falls as it is down here?

Yvette: No. And you can keep it. I've already had to dig my truck out of a snowbank twice this winter.

Alex: Time to break out the skidoo

Yvette: I tossed a pair of skis in the back of my truck as emergency backup.

Alex: Not snowshoes?

Yvette: I have those as well. Plus emergency food, flares, and the rest of it.

Alex: You're a regular Boy Scout. I volunteer to be trapped in the wilderness with you anytime.

Yvette: Were you ever a Boy Scout?

Alex: For one week. Then I got the bright idea of booby trapping all the doors in the gymnasium with water balloons. Our grand poohbah wasn't very pleased, and I ended up sent home.

Yvette: That seems harsh. Your scoutmaster overreacted.

Alex: I'd added dye to the water to make it look more intimidating. It seems purple wasn't one of his favourite colours.

Yvette: You didn't.

Alex: It was okay. My dad ended up running our own version of Boy Scouts when the next crew of foster kids came through. I still got my camping badge. The home version.

Yvette: You'll have to tell me more when we see each other tomorrow.

Alex: Deal. Only, after we win the gaudy sweater contest, right?

Yvette: Absolutely. Brooke and Mack are going down.

ALEX FOUND himself grinning as he flipped back through the various text messages he and Yvette had exchanged over the past couple of days.

Wednesday morning, snow was still falling, but he had done what he needed to for Silver Stone ranch. He was just killing time, waiting for some final paperwork to be signed and for Ashton to get his ass back in the truck.

The older man stood outside the office door, hands in his

pockets, head nodding as he chatted with the local ranch foreman, obviously not in a rush to get anywhere.

Alex's phone rang, and he answered it, eager for the distraction.

"Hey, Dad. What's happening?"

"Hi. Your mom and I were sitting here having a cup of coffee and decided to take a chance that you might be free to chat. Got a minute? I've got you on speaker phone."

Alex glanced over, but Ashton hadn't moved an inch. "I can talk."

"How are things going? How are things with that girl you said you liked?"

For fuck's sake. It was like he was twelve years old. "Girl? Come on, Dad. She's nearly thirty. I'm the same."

"You're just babies," his dad rattled.

"Speaking of babies, are you being careful?" His mother. Of course.

Even on the phone, and miles away, Alex was still instantly ready to nope out of this conversation. Redirection, now.

"How are you both?" Alex asked, pointedly changing the topic. "Cait taking care of you okay? And Aaron?" His foster sister and her husband.

"Your sister and Aaron are being wonderful. Plus, Davis is home as well."

"Davis?" Shit. His foster brother's name was unexpected news. "What's he doing around?"

"Helping." His father's tone was no longer amused. "I know he's had his moments, but he came back and apologized. He's making up for his mistakes."

"He left town with a warrant for his arrest hanging over his head, Dad. That's not a *moment*. That's a major fuckup."

"Language," his mother warned. "And I agree with you. He was an ass."

"So why's he there?" Alex was ready to jump in his truck

and drive across the prairies to plant a fist in his brother's face if necessary.

His mom sighed. "Because he realized he was an ass, and he apologized for being an ass, and he's working hard to no longer be an ass."

"Language, darling," Alex's father rumbled, amusement in his voice before speaking again to Alex. "Son, we've talked about this before. When a man takes a wrong step, you don't push him farther off a cliff. You give him a solid path to walk on and then shove him in the right direction."

A philosophy Alex agreed with completely, having been on the receiving end of his parents tough-yet-sweet love many times over the years. "I know, and you're right. You just caught me off guard." He took a moment to get his head together before starting up again. "If you say things are going well, that's good. I'll trust you to let me know if that changes and you need me to come home again."

"Of course. But that won't be necessary," his mom insisted. "Honey, you need time to get your life happening. We're okay right now. Taking it easy, letting ourselves heal."

"I promise Davis is pulling more than his fair share. In fact, I'll get him to give you a call, okay? He mentioned he was going to. Probably was worried you'd bite his head off, though." Dad coughed pointedly. "We don't have to worry about that now, do we?"

"No. I'll be good. Tell the jerk to get in touch." Alex could picture his parents. Sitting at the kitchen table, mugs in front of them. "How is physical rehab? Still tough?"

"Very." His mom chuckled. "I'm very thankful my trainer is easy on the eyes. So, there's that."

"Mom." Alex chuckled. "You're terrible."

"She's incorrigible," his dad corrected. "But what makes it worse is she's right, and she keeps teasing me about it. Your mom got this gorgeous, dark-haired beauty. I'm stuck with an old guy nearly my age. Not even a pretty girl to make me do my exercises."

"Truly, life isn't fair." Alex noticed motion by the barn as Ashton shook hands farewell then turned to make his way to the truck. "Love you both, but I need to cut this short. Give Cait and Aaron a hug from me. Tell Davis to call. I'll talk with you in a week if all is well."

"We love you," they said in near-perfect chorus.

Alex hung up, just a trace of discomfort edging into the satisfaction of knowing his parents were doing okay.

Ashton pulled open the door and eyed Alex with displeasure. "I didn't call shotgun."

"Consider me your chauffeur," Alex encouraged. "Also, I got here first. I'm driving."

A solid snort escaped Ashton as he buckled up. "Fine, just don't put us in a ditch."

"Yes, sir." Alex gave a wave to the cowboy waiting to slide the gate open in front of them then headed the truck and trailer out onto the highway. "Some nice-looking animals we picked up."

"Yup. Don't agree with everything Frank does, but it's clear the Stone family knows horses right down to their roots." Silver Stone's award-winning bloodlines were a bit of luck and a whole lot of hard work, especially on Luke Stone's part.

"Family's like that sometimes," Alex said dryly, thinking about Davis. "You take the good and try and focus on it, hoping it outweighs the bad."

A low rumble of agreement. "How are your parents?"

Alex smiled. "Was just talking to them. They're nearly done with the physio part of recovery. Seems to be going well."

Ashton dipped his chin. "Hell of a thing, the two of them ending up in surgery at the same time."

"Once you're on the list, it's not something that you want to put off when you get a chance to take it." Alex glanced at his foreman. "What about you and your family? Seems to be a good thing to have Tucker underfoot."

For the first time, he got a full-out grin from the old man. "I'm glad my nephew agreed to come apprentice with me. He came to visit every summer since he was a little tyke. Didn't realize how much fun it would be to have a grown-up family member to boss around."

Alex laughed. Tucker was one step away from taking over Ashton's job, and it was good to know there were no hard feelings with that soon-to-occur transition.

Which triggered another thought. "You plan on retiring once Tucker takes over?"

An answer he figured was going to be *hell no*.

"Might try and find something else to keep me busy," Ashton said easily.

Well, hell. Maybe it was time to push his luck. "Maybe you should try and find some*body* to spend some of that busy time with. You know, someone sweet who loves animals."

"You mind your own damn business," Ashton warned, but amusement laced his voice.

"I never mind my own damn business. It's one of my charms," Alex pointed out. He glanced to the side. "At the risk of being too blunt, why the hell are you and Sonora sneaking around behind closed doors?"

Ashton met his gaze for a brief second before Alex had to look back at the road. But that moment and the expression on the other man's face had been enough to make it clear.

The sneaking wasn't Ashton's idea.

"I'm working on it," he grumbled. Then he sat back and stared straight ahead. "If you repeat that to anyone, I will deny it vehemently. Then I will put you on night shift for the rest of the month. Which would be a shitty thing to do to that sweet thing you're making the moves on."

"Damn if you don't play mean," Alex complained.

"When you've been in the game for as long as I have, you know when it's time to stop messing around." Ashton tipped his hat over his eyes. "Happy driving. Wake me when we get home."

Which left Alex alone with his thoughts for the next two hours. A lot of thoughts, all down wildly diverse paths.

Ashton was making a move for Sonora. Interesting.

His parents were recovering well, and his foster brother— one of them—was hanging around and helping.

Back at home, Yvette had been sending him sweet, interesting messages for the past three days. Despite that, he still missed the hell out of her.

Which made for one tangled mess of thoughts, running on an endless loop in his brain.

Yet he couldn't get upset about it. They were all good things, really, and when it came down to it, they were all bits of an adventure that he had longed for.

The journey was part of the destination. He didn't want to wish away a single minute.

7

_____

Of course. Wednesday would turn out to be a day from hell. Snow had started falling at four twenty-seven a.m.—Yvette knew the precise time because she was already up, headed out on an emergency callout.

The three farms she visited before noon all had turned into one adrenaline-drenched moment after another. She was chased by a bull, squished against the wooden stall sidewall by an overeager horse, and came within inches of being tossed out of the hayloft when an owl unexpectedly swooped past her and frightened the farmer into bolting straight into her.

At the time she was supposed to be headed home to get ready for the firefighters' annual Christmas gathering, Yvette was stuck ankle deep in icy muck.

She hauled herself free, waved goodbye to the poor farmer who still had to complete all his chores, and hauled out her phone so she could touch base with Alex.

Normally, she would've been beside herself, worrying about being late and what he would think about her lack of responsibility. It was terrible that she could hear her mother's voice lecturing her again on personal commitment and thinking of others first.

It didn't help that over the past couple of days, she'd fielded a series of text messages from her siblings. She must have been the topic of conversation during the Saturday family dinner, and who knows what her mother had shared, because her three older brothers all sent *if you need help, just ask* messages. Which would have been sweet, except their help came with caveats and a demand that she move back to Regina.

Carrie, on the other hand, had started by accusing Yvette of not coming to the dinner because she was jealous then worked her way to forgiving her baby sister "who I love so much and just want the best for." All without Yvette once texting back.

Yvette pulled up Alex's contact and forced back all the negative thoughts. She was *late*—these things happened during the course of a workday, especially for someone who dealt with animals.

She'd taken the time over the past couple days to think hard, especially in light of how the nasty texts had made her feel.

Jumping to conclusions and assuming the worst of *good* people were both bad habits of hers that needed to stop, which meant right now she needed to trust Alex would understand.

He answered as if he'd been waiting for her call. "Hey, gorgeous."

"If you could see me right now? You'd use a different word." With the heat on full, whatever was stuck to the bottom of her boots was warming up and filling the cab with a terrible aroma. "Scratch that. If you could smell me right now—we'd have a problem."

He caught her hidden message, and he chuckled. "Running late from a job?"

"You do not want me to join a party right now. Not unless you need the room cleared."

"Remember, half of us have lost our sense of smell in the first place," Alex assured her. "But don't worry. Head home. Wash up. I'll wait outside your place until you're ready."

"Let me meet you at the fire hall," Yvette counteroffered. "It's still a date, and you can drive me home if you want to do the good-night kiss on the doorstep, but I'd feel better if you were already enjoying time with your friends. I promise to get there as quick as I can."

He hesitated for a moment before agreeing. "Park in the back, and come around the south side of the building. Call me when you get here, and I'll meet you. We have to get our sweaters on, after all."

"Our winning sweaters," she assured him.

"That's my girl."

She hung up with a warm glow coasting through her from her filthy toes all the way to the ends of her tangled hair.

Scrubbing up didn't take long, especially since she could barely stand the smell of herself. She sent Alex a quick message when she pulled into the parking lot at the back of the fire hall. Christmas lights in every window turned the place festive, and the building looked as if it had shining eyes and a gleaming smile.

She rounded the corner of the building and pulled to a stop.

A snowman blocked her way. Not just one, but a veritable army. Some of them standing, some of them lying down. She strolled forward, amusement rising as she realized it was a reenactment of a zombie apocalypse, snow version.

She was staring around in amazement when a strong arm looped around her waist, Alex pulling her close. "Hey."

"Hey." She slipped her arms around his neck without thinking. "Oops. This kind of feels like what I'm supposed to be doing right now."

"Not a problem with me," he whispered as he leaned in

slowly, gaze locked on her lips. "As long as the next thing you're supposed to do is kiss me."

"I can do—" Her words cut off as he pressed their lips together.

Short, but definitely not sweet. Her heart pounded when he finally let her go.

His grin was firmly in place as he gestured to the side yard. "Like them?"

"The snowmen? They're cute." Yvette glanced to the side to examine them closer. "Did you make them?"

"Me and a bunch of the guys. Come on, I need to show you the best part." He led her down a well-stomped path to where the biggest mass of snowmen gathered in a thick huddle.

All different heights, with very individual characters, the snowmen were arranged in a perfect half circle around a bench. Arms reaching skyward, some of them as if they were doing jazz hands. All of them with eyes and carrot noses grinning toward the centre as if staring at something important.

Alex held out his hands in his best Vanna White imitation. "Ta-da. Our selfie station."

One snowman tilted slightly, coming to lean against his neighbour. Their two heads clumped together, noses crossing like swords. She could've sworn they were trying to kiss each other.

Laughter started deep in her belly, welling upward along with contentment. "It's perfect."

Alex slipped her fingers into his. "Come on. We need to get our sweaters on and go impress people."

"Also, I'm starving," Yvette said quickly. "Can we impress people while we eat?"

He hummed as if considering. "I don't know. Can you eat without holding your plate in front of the wonder that is our gaudiness?"

"This is your warning that I require food at regular intervals."

"I hear you."

He pulled her into the warmth of the hall, laughter and the scent of Christmas wrapping around them.

A moment later, his arms were wrapped around her as well. He leaned in and kissed her again. Deep and slow and distracting. She could've stayed there for a long time, enjoying his lips on hers.

Except for the growl that escaped her stomach, echoing off the walls loud enough to send him snickering.

He eased away, smiling into her embarrassed face. "That sounds dangerous to ignore."

She reached into the bag hanging off her shoulder. "Here. If we slip them on now, we can head upstairs and join the chow line. Perfect timing."

The cardigans went on, the LED lights switched to high. Between the two of them, they damn near glowed as they went up the steps hand-in-hand.

A cheer rose as they hit the top landing. The crowd that had gathered was bigger than the year before, with all the volunteer firefighters and their families in attendance.

The fire chief rose to his feet. Brad eyed them both, his grin widening. "Well, don't you two brighten up the place."

"Not too shabby yourself there, Chief," Alex returned, sliding his arm around Yvette's waist and guiding her to the tail end of the buffet line. "We'll be over in a minute."

Yvette was still blinking. "Is he sparkling?"

Brad's sweater seemed to be made entirely of strands of tinsel, the layers waving under the bright overhead lights like a black-and-white aurora borealis.

"Don't worry. His sweater is good, but ours are better," Alex assured her. He grabbed her a plate and handed it over. He leaned in close and spoke with a conspiratorial quiet as they started their way past the tables groaning with plates of turkey, fresh-baked buns, and all sorts of salads. "Let me know which is your favourite dessert, and I'll nab you an extra."

"Dessert?"

He tilted his head to the far counter. "*Shhhhh*. Don't let the hordes know they're there."

Yvette's mouth watered as she layered mashed potatoes, meatballs, and gravy on her plate, accompanied by a hearty scoop of cranberry sauce. "I need basic goodness right now. Lots of it."

She had no idea how he managed it, but when she put her plate on the table in the open spot next to Brooke, Alex plopped another plate heaped high with everything she'd already selected. "Here. You need to keep your strength up."

She was about to protest. Her brain did an unwelcome objection at the sheer volume of food in front of her. But Alex's gaze was steady on hers.

"It was a busy day. Thanks."

He leaned in and touched their noses together for a sheer second, amusement dancing in his eyes. "Eat what you want. I promise there will be dessert in your future."

"Alex. What's this madness you've created outside?" Ryan and Madison sat opposite them, and as the two of them teased Alex about the snowmen, Yvette dug into her food.

Beside her, Brooke leaned their shoulders together, speaking softly. "Keep eating. I heard you went from one end of the county to the other today, and I bet you never stopped for lunch." Her friend nabbed the bun off Yvette's plate. A moment later she had it buttered thickly and returned. "Besides, if you're eating, that means I get to tell you all sorts of things and you can't respond. Because you're far too polite to talk with your mouth full."

Yvette glanced at her briefly, timing her swallow so she could take a quick drink of her pop before sticking out her tongue. "I am capable of eating quickly and giving you hell. If you deserve it."

"I deserve nothing of the sort," Brooke insisted. Her volume dropped again. "I see Alex is being a sweetheart."

Yvette stabbed another piece of turkey and swirled it in her gravy. "*La la la la la.*"

A laugh escaped her friend. "You're happy. You deserve to be, and while I know he's had his moments, Alex is looking out for you. I like it."

That made two of them. Yvette broke off a chunk of bun and swirled it in the gravy on her plate. She paused before popping it in her mouth and met Brooke's gaze. "I'm having fun, and I'm learning things."

She was thinking about the changes she'd realized needed to happen.

Only, her friend's brain went down an entirely different route. Brooke outright snorted. "Well, good, and what exactly are you being schooled about? Oh, I know. You're learning naughty, dirty things because Alex is teaching you—"

"Stop," Yvette said, but it came out muffled because of the damn piece of bun in her mouth. She chewed and swallowed quickly. "No."

"Well, if you do learn something new and naughty, the friend code says you have to tell me. Since I'm your bestie and all."

"I'm eating," Yvette complained. "Don't ask me that now."

"That's okay. I'll ask him," Brooke said suddenly as she leaned forward and, before Yvette could protest, spoke louder. "Right, Alex?"

He interrupted the conversation he was having with their friends across the table to glance their direction. His gaze met Yvette's. He must've seen a clue in her eyes that what they were talking about was a little less innocent than stealing extra desserts, because he grinned widely. "Definitely right. Right away, right now, and right as rain. Don't know what you're talking about, but I'm fully on board."

Her cheeks flushed red hot. Oh, boy.

~

THESE WERE the moments that made it so clear to Alex that he and Yvette belonged together.

Yeah, she was embarrassed as all get out, but as he stole his hand under the table and caught her fingers in his, squeezing them tight before resting their joined hands on his thigh, it was a *good* embarrassed.

He still had some tangles to unfurl when it came to this woman. But the pieces that were lining up perfectly made him not just tingle with need but soothed and satisfied something inside him. He knew they had to be friends first.

On the other side of Yvette, Brooke was wearing the kind of smile that meant trouble. "I like an agreeable man."

Her husband sat across the table from her. Mack eyed her with anticipation in his gaze. "Oh, you do. And you have one. So stop teasing my friend."

"Alex is my friend too," Brooke complained. "Which means I get to tease him as well as Yvette."

Madison got in on the action. She'd pushed away from the table, hands resting on the swell of her belly. "Teasing is what you do best, but it's time we deal with the really big elephant in the room."

Mack slapped a hand over his mouth and shook his head, his eyes crinkled up with amusement.

"You are *so* annoying," Madison said as she slapped him lightly on the arm.

"I never said anything," Mack complained indignantly.

"You were thinking it. Really loudly." Madison eased against Ryan's side. "Make your friend be nice to me."

"Stop thinking terrible things about Madison's baby belly," Ryan ordered, slipping his hand over the swell and pressing a kiss to her cheek. "It's beautiful."

"Thank you, darling." She laid her hand on top of his and spoke softly, amusement in her tone. "Okay, it's beautiful *and* big."

"It absolutely is—the beautiful part. That's what I planned to say before you added anything." Mack reached a hand across the table to Brooke. "Can you help me out here, babe? Before they throw me out a window or something?"

She caught his fingers and nodded briefly. "The floor is all yours."

Yvette's fingers tightened as Alex's suspicion shot to high. The setup was perfect for a certain kind of announcement.

Sure enough, Mack glanced down the table to make sure their core group members were all listening. "Brooke and I are pleased to announce she too will be doing the beautiful belly thing. Baby Klassen is expected to arrive this coming summer."

Which meant the next ten minutes were taken up with hugs and handshakes and firm back poundings as the news spread.

Yvette got in the first hug with Brooke before shaking her head in disbelief. "I didn't suspect a thing. So happy for you."

Brooke winked at Alex as she leaned over Yvette's shoulder. "We had to wait until there was a big enough crowd to make our announcement worthwhile."

"Fantastic news," Alex said as he slipped in behind Yvette and squeezed Brooke carefully. "You and Mack are going to rock the family thing."

"It will help that we have so many babysitters around," Brooke said with a wink before turning to the next person to accept their congratulations.

Alex slid his arm back around Yvette and led her around the table so they could join the group congratulating Mack.

Then they stepped aside, waiting with Brad and Hanna for

a lull in the action. Yvette leaned against Alex's chest, totally at ease.

He liked it. He liked it a lot.

She jerked upright, glancing back at him before tilting her head excitedly across the room. "Come with me. I see someone I need to talk to."

He went willingly, coming to a stop with her in front of a petite redhead who appeared to be attempting to inch away from the man who had her trapped.

Yvette cleared her throat. "Sorry to interrupt."

The man—a brother of one of their volunteers?—glared at her because she had totally cut him off midsentence.

But the woman turned with a grateful smile. "No problem. What's up?"

"Brad told me you had some information I need. It'll just take a minute. Thanks so much, so nice to meet you," Yvette said to the man even as she caught the woman by the arm and, still hanging on to Alex, dragged the two of them to the side of the room.

The man stared after them, confusion and a touch of frustration on his face.

"Thank you," the woman said, laying her hand on Yvette's arm and squeezing tightly. "He's a new volunteer, so I didn't want to kick his butt, but it was getting close."

"I was lying about the Brad thing," Yvette said. "I do need to talk to you, though." She turned to Alex. "Have you met Sydney since you got back to town? I don't think she was living local when you left."

The name sounded familiar, but he shook his head, holding out a hand. "Alex Thorne. Silver Stone ranch hand and one of the coordinators here at the hall."

"You're Alex." The woman smiled brightly. She gave his hand a firm shake then rested her hands on her hips. "Dr.

Sydney Jeremiah. I was based out of Black Diamond, but I'm opening a care center here in Heart Falls."

Now Alex had a face to put with the name. "I have heard of you. I've been fortunate enough to not have needed your services."

"Let's hope it stays that way," she said cheerfully before turning to Yvette. "Yes?"

"Do you do house calls?"

Sydney looked Yvette up and down, gaze lingering on the lights on both their sweaters.

Yvette shook her head. "Not for me. Creighton Reiner injured his foot. He let me stitch him up, but it would be good if you took a look at my embroidery."

Sydney nodded slowly. "I assume this is one of the local old-timers?"

She hadn't asked for his help, but Alex was more than willing to offer it. "Bit of a cranky bastard, but he's got a good heart. If you want, I can accompany you and Yvette when you've got time. See if I can help things go a little smoother."

Yvette bumped her shoulder into his. "That's a good idea."

The doctor shrugged. "I'll check my calendar. Even cranky old bastards deserve medical attention."

"Thanks." Yvette tilted her head toward where Brad had just called for them to gather. "Come with us if you want safety in numbers. You know, to avoid your stalker."

"The guy was just being overly friendly," Sydney said before wrinkling her nose. "Kind of like a puppy, but I didn't have a rolled-up newspaper to bop him on the nose with."

Alex snickered and offered them both his arms. When they both slipped hands around his biceps, he marched them toward the crowd, feeling like a hero.

"It is time for the official first-ever gaudy sweater contest." Someone had gotten Madison a microphone, and she stood on the raised platform at the side of the room, one hand unconsciously balanced on top of her belly. "Because we all know that last year's unofficial event was won by my husband. Thank you very much."

"He was the only one who dressed up," Mack shouted.

"You snooze, you lose," Ryan returned.

Sydney slipped away into the group. Yvette shocked the hell out of Alex by curling her arm around his waist so they stood side by side, most definitely a tangled-together couple.

While Madison went over the rules for voting, Yvette leaned her cheek against Alex's and whispered in his ear. "Whether we win or lose, I really enjoyed doing up the sweaters. And spending time with you. I wanted you to know that."

He kissed the corner of her mouth quickly, pulling back until he could rest their foreheads together. "Thank you for being a good sport. I think we're doing a fine job of this dating thing."

"I guess we are."

"Plus, we're totally going to win." He winked before turning back to the crowd.

A moment later, everyone who was dressed appropriately slid to the front of the gathering then turned to face the audience.

"I need the judges to step forward, please," Madison announced.

A group of a dozen giggling children squirmed their way to the front.

From then on, the contest was pretty much a shoe-in. Brooke and Mack had decorated their sweaters with row upon row of shiny, ribbon-wrapped boxes. Ryan was once again wearing the classic cardigan that he and Madison used during their battle. Brad had his shimmering tinsel coat, and Hanna one that was covered with greenery. Mistletoe, maybe?

Alex needed to tease Brad about that particular choice at some future private moment.

Another dozen of the volunteers had put their hand in as well, but when he and Yvette trailed in front of the children, their eyes truly lit up. Especially when he handed one of them a finger puppet cow out of his pocket. "You decide where he goes. Want to put him in the barn?"

The little girl's eyes glowed. She shook her head and very carefully pushed the beast against the piece of Velcro on top of one of the fence posts. Giggles ensued from the cast of judges.

A moment later he and Yvette were both surrounded as eager children took their finger puppets and went to town. All the little spots of Velcro that were randomly placed over the cardigan were filled with farm animals in most nonsensical places. Most of them standing on their heads because that seemed to bring the greatest delight.

But it was the little girl who had both the man farmer and woman farmer who got the most laughs. She'd decided that the two of them needed to sit at the very peak of the barn on the back of Yvette's sweater.

The only way it would work was to wrap them up in each other's arms. The little tyke patted her hand firmly to make sure they stayed in place.

"There," she said. "They're like the star at the top of the tree. That's what makes it perfect, you know."

The two tangled up together, sitting and looking out over a wonderful home? Alex couldn't agree more.

When the children had finished voting, he and Yvette had clearly won.

Brad tried to look stern, but there was too much Christmas cheer in the room for it to stick. He mock grumbled as he stepped beside Alex. "You found out the kids were judging."

Alex shrugged. "Maybe. Maybe not."

A soft snicker escaped Yvette. Alex ignored everyone around them so he could lead her downstairs to the place of honour under the watchful eyes of the zombie snowmen.

There they sat, arms wrapped around each other as the official photo of the winning gaudy sweater was taken for prosperity.

Before giving up their spot, they took a couple of selfies. Then Alex took Yvette back into the hall to enjoy the laughter and warmth of good friends.

One more successful step toward the future.

8

*W*hen Yvette opened the day-ten drawer, she found—as usual—the next day's key. But the actual present wasn't shiny like the tiny horse charm that had been in the day-nine drawer. It wasn't sweet and delicious like the day-seven coupon for a box of Timbits.

It was far more mysterious and made her heart pound. A thin cylinder just slightly larger than a pencil unscrewed to reveal what appeared to be an antique treasure map.

She squealed with delight, allowing happiness to pump through her thoroughly before picking up her phone and messaging Alex.

Yvette: There's only one problem with today's present
Alex: Oh?
Yvette: I don't seem to see where I need to start this adventure. Can I have a clue? I thought about checking to see if you used invisible ink, but I don't want to ruin the map if I don't have to.
Alex: You might need a partner to deal with this problem. I understand you're coming out to Silver Stone today. Maybe we can take a break when you're done.

Oh, that tricky man. Yvette glanced over the map again, mentally overlaying the path of the footsteps in the directions over what she remembered of Silver Stone.

Yvette: Deal. I'll try to give you a heads-up about half an hour before I'm done.

As it turned out, she didn't need to worry. Alex met her in the parking area, cowboy hat in place, working boots on his feet.

"Are you my guide today?" she asked.

He sauntered forward. "Didn't even have to volunteer. Ashton put me on veterinarian duty straight off."

She paused before glancing around and deciding *to hell with it*. "You plan to give me a kiss?"

Immediately, he pulled off his hat and an instant later she was wrapped up in his arms, his big hand bracing the back of her head. "Didn't want to scare you, but can't say I was eager to skip this."

Before she could tease back, he'd pulled her in even tighter, igniting her senses with a brief but enthusiastic kiss.

He stepped back and replaced his hat, tilting it forward and giving it a tap before grinning at her. He tilted his head toward the second barn. "This way."

This was not an area where they'd ever had problems. Yvette enjoyed working with Alex. Enjoyed the way that, as they approached each new animal, he would give a clear rundown on what the issues were, but even as he was talking, he would slow his step. Lower his voice so that when she went to check the animal, the beast was as calm as possible.

They stopped after a couple of hours and headed into the mess hall for a coffee break. Yvette pulled out the treasure map and placed it on the table between them. "This is fun. Once you mentioned you were going to be my guide, I had a pretty good idea of where we need to start."

"Sounds good to me. We only have a couple more jobs on the list."

Which is how, not even an hour later, they ended up standing beside the main door of the oldest building on Silver Stone. A connection between the two newer builds, the aged wood was honey gold in places where hands had touched over years and years of wear.

Yvette glanced at the map. "Twenty paces south."

That clue was easy. It led them straight down a corridor with stalls on one side and tack rooms and other storage spaces on the opposite.

The next part wasn't so clear. When she hesitated, Alex leaned over her. "Now what, sweetheart?"

"Now it looks like a spring. Or spiral. But I have no idea what that means." She glanced around, slowly pivoting in the hopes she'd see something that would trigger an idea.

"Let me know when you want another clue," Alex offered.

"Right now would be good."

He dipped his chin slowly. "I require payment for my clues."

A very unladylike snort escaped Yvette. "Of course you do."

He eased her against him. "Don't worry. I won't bankrupt you."

Her lips were being taken again, and Yvette wondered how on earth she had survived this long without Alex's kisses. They were delicious. Mesmerizing, soul-satisfying, and addictive.

Breathtaking as well, apparently, because when he pulled away, she clung to his shoulders to keep on her feet. "You do that too many times, I'm going to puddle onto the floor."

"Going to be hard to find your treasure if you turn into an amoeba." He tapped her nose then twirled a finger in the air by his shoulder. "Here's a clue."

Yvette watched closely, but while she could see the motion, it didn't trigger any other—

His hand slowly rose in the air.

"There's a second story, isn't there?" Yvette demanded, looking around to see how to access it.

On the wall a few feet away, a set of ropes were looped on a hook. They led skyward toward pulleys high in the rafters.

Okay. Clue solved, but there was no way in hell Yvette was using some old-fashioned dumbwaiter system to get into the loft. "Tell me there's another way up."

Alex had the ropes and was lowering something toward them. "It's safe," he promised. "I checked everything."

Her heart pounded, and this time it wasn't from the excitement of the search. "*Alex.*"

Every bit of her fear came out in the word.

He wrapped his arm around her and gave her another squeeze before gesturing toward the contraption. A three-by-three-foot platform hung at swing height off the floor. "I'll ride with you. I'll be with you every step of the way."

A long, unsteady breath escaped her, and Yvette stared into his face. His lips still held the faintest hint of a smile—it didn't seem as if he ever lost that. But his eyes were serious, and he stood rock solid. Like an immovable mountain.

A steady place to put her trust.

"Don't drop me," she whispered before easing her butt back onto the platform.

He leaned forward and looked her straight in the eye. "It'll be fun. Trust me."

The entire base under her hips sank an inch when he joined her, and a little shriek involuntarily escaped.

The next thing she knew, he was pulling the ropes and lifting them skyward hand over hand. They had left their coats hanging on a wall just inside the barn, and now she watched as his biceps and forearms flexed with the sheer brute strength he used on every motion.

Dear God, his arms were the sexiest thing she'd seen in her life.

They were also the most distracting thing she'd ever seen, apparently, because the next thing she knew, he'd pulled on a third rope and swung their platform over the solid wooden floor of the loft.

Yvette slipped her feet to the floorboards, and Alex joined her, tossing the ropes over a hook beside the nearest beam.

Then he held her in his arms again, pressing a tender kiss to her forehead. "Didn't mean to scare you. But thank you for the gift you just gave me."

She stilled, considering his words. When she looked up, it was to see absolute truth in his eyes. She drowned in it for a moment. In this amazing and none-too-familiar sensation. She hadn't been perfect, and yet he didn't seem displeased at all with her. He hadn't teased or made rude comments or anything.

He'd thanked her for her gift—trusting him.

The moment was huge, and yet she wasn't quite ready to acknowledge that out loud.

Instead, she dipped her chin briefly then pulled the map from her pocket. "Not much farther. Want to help me find the treasure?"

He winked and gestured her toward the hay bales. "Happy hunting."

Less than five minutes of crawling this direction then that, Yvette let out a burst of laughter. "No way."

Tucked into the far corner left of the loft, the hay bales had been moved to create a cozy little hollow with a thick, brightly coloured picnic blanket as a base.

Alex made himself at home, stretching out on the sturdy

cotton surface. He patted the space next to him. "Come here. I have something for you."

She couldn't resist and crawled beside him, leaning up on one elbow. "I bet you do."

He stroked his knuckles over her cheek. "Surprise. The picnic blanket is yours."

She glanced down in happy surprise. "It's beautiful."

"It's got a sturdy jean fabric on the backside with a triple layer of batting, so it's straw and hay durable," he said with a smile. "Since we both know fooling around anywhere near such substances is a recipe for disaster."

"Were we planning on fooling around?" she asked innocently.

"We're planning on doing whatever makes us happy." His cowboy hat tumbled to the side as Alex slid sideways until Yvette lay flat on her back. He gazed down with hunger in his eyes.

Doing anything sexual in a barn where she worked was not part of her standard operating procedure, but focusing on what would make her happy right now was very enticing. "Kiss me?"

He tossed his cowboy hat farther and adjusted himself so that the entire long, lean length of him pressed against her side. He leaned over, lips inches from hers. "Yes, ma'am."

SHE WAS SO SWEET. The contrast between her being absolutely fearless and totally in control to these moments when she showed delicacy and fear. The veterinarian who knew her shit and the woman who still seemed to be finding her feet at times. He loved all of it. How all her components wrapped together to create a woman who rocked his socks off.

Also, touching her, even the slightest bit, made his cock harder than fucking stone.

He cursed inside, because she was setting the pace. He'd said it was totally up to her how fast and how far—and he meant to keep that promise, but dear *God,* did he want her.

Right now, though, he was going to take that first taste a little further. Resting his hand on her waistline, he put their lips together. They'd practiced this part enough over the past week that she automatically lifted her arms to wrap around him. Sliding the fingers of one hand into his hair and arching into him as he slid his hand slowly up her belly.

He teased their tongues together, her breath escaping in teeny pants that rushed past his cheek. She gasped when his hand landed on her breast.

Alex groaned before he could stop himself. Even through her thick shirt and bra, the heat of her overflowing his palm lit a bonfire inside him.

Floorboards creaked. A steady, sharp rhythm followed—

Footsteps.

Growing closer.

"*Shit.*"

They scrambled apart. Yvette tugged at her shirt to pull it back over her assets while Alex rearranged himself to keep from cutting off all feeling in his cock. They both stayed seated, hidden behind the bales.

"We should probably use up the hay in the second barn loft first." Tucker's voice. Deep, with a hint of laughter at the edges.

Alex was sure they were out of sight. Yvette had pressed her fingers over her mouth, so they were silent even as they exchanged amused glances.

But Alex also figured Tucker totally had their number and knew they were there. Now to see if they got busted or if the man waited until later to give Alex hell for fooling around in the loft.

"I thought this barn still held enough to last a couple

months. But you don't want to use it now?" Ginny Stone, Tucker's fiancée, made a *huh* sound. "That makes no sense."

"Keeping spaces open for...*cats*...to play is important." Tucker said it dryly.

For some reason Tucker's comment got a huge laugh out of Ginny. "Okay, fine. Don't know why you brought me up here then."

"You don't? Let me refresh your memory, goddess."

A sudden gasp from Ginny was followed by more laughter, then one set of footsteps moved toward the far-*right* corner of the loft.

Away from where Alex and Yvette sat motionless.

No time to lose, because there were some things Alex didn't need to hear. His future boss fooling around was one of them.

Alex pressed a finger over his lips, tilting his head to the exit. Yvette followed him, scooping up the blanket and silently moving on his heels until they were at the edge of the loft.

"How do we...?" she whispered.

He pointed to the side wall, stepping around it to where a narrow but very sturdy set of stairs descended.

They didn't say anything until they were all the way outside. Then Yvette laughed, softly punching Alex in the biceps. "There was another way up into the loft."

"There are many ways to find treasure," he teased back. "Can't turn down a magical carpet ride for plain-Jane stairs, now could you?"

She shook her head, glanced around quick, then kissed him. "That was fun. Thanks for the blanket as well."

He grinned. "I should get back to work. See you tomorrow, though?"

"You bet."

He walked her to her truck, stole another kiss, and waited until her truck disappeared off the ranch before forcing his feet back into work mode. Eager for the day to be done and the next to arrive.

Hᵉ Wẇẉ Sẏṷṷẇẉ ṷẄẋṷṷ when Yvette picked him up at eight a.m.

Sydney Jeremiah was already sitting in the passenger seat, and she immediately slid into the middle, juggling coffees as Alex got himself settled and buckled in.

"We could take my crew cab," Alex pointed out.

"I figured if Creighton sees my truck coming, he might not bundle himself off and hide." Yvette pointed to the bags on the front dash. "My turn to pick up cinnamon buns. Tansy and Rose said to say hi, by the way."

Sydney helped by passing Alex a treat then held the bag as a plate for Yvette to grab hers from once they were out on the highway. "Is it terrible if I confess Buns and Roses is one of the main reasons I made the move to Heart Falls?"

"That's not terrible. Shows you got sense," Alex assured her.

Yvette grinned. "The coffee shop is near and dear to everyone's heart, but I have to confess that Rose and all of the trinkets she sells make me just as happy."

"You like sparkly things?" Sydney asked.

Alex met Yvette's gaze briefly before she focused back on the highway. "A little too much, sometimes," she confessed.

"Well, that's not possible." Sydney took a long drink of her coffee before sighing happily. "Unless you've got a hoarding issue that I need to support you in correcting."

Alex was quick to speak in Yvette's defense. "Definitely not hoarding, but you need to stop by sometime and see all the cool stuff she's collected. Heck, I still need to take a thorough look. There's a lot of neat collectibles in her home."

"What's your favourite?" Sydney asked seriously.

Yvette barely hesitated before cracking a grin. "Well, before this month, I would have said my sand collection, which isn't so much shiny as very personal. Every time I've hit a beach, or a lake with a beach, I steal away just enough to put in a little tube. They're all in a display case. It's fascinating to see all the different textures and colours."

"That does sound amazing. I can see that bringing back a lot of happy memories. Good for you." Sydney licked her fingers clean before asking, "What's your new favourite?"

Alex liked this woman who was smart and sharp and keen to encourage Yvette.

A low hum escaped Yvette. "My new favourite is courtesy of that gentleman in the passenger seat beside you. He's been giving me pretty charms to put on a bracelet."

Sydney gave him a friendly nudge in the ribs with her elbow. "Way to go, charmer. It's nice to see a couple get along as well as you two do. How long have you been dating?"

"What's the date today?" Yvette said, a smile curling her lips.

Sydney looked confused for a minute before Alex took pity on her. "Took a while to get my head out of my ass and be smart enough to realize what a gem Yvette is. Then I was out of town until the start of this month."

Shock briefly flickered in the woman's eyes before she put on her game face. "Good for you."

Conversation slipped into discussing other places in town and where Sydney might be able to find someone to help with some construction items. Alex sang along when "Run Run Rudolph" came on the playlist, and the girls laughed as he hammed it up along with Luke Bryan.

Yvette shook her head, though. "I seem to remember you once said you only sang during karaoke nights."

"That would be a pity. You've got a great voice." Sydney nodded approvingly.

"Always have enjoyed singing along with the radio." Alex wasn't about to confess that after deciding to pursue Yvette, he'd realized singing was another thing they could do together. He hadn't thought of it in time to add anything musical to her calendar gifts, but he was already plotting future mischief.

Mischief that involved her and him and some great love songs. Just to keep the mood rolling in the right direction.

The bumpy road up to the farm smoothed slightly as they pulled into the yard.

"Looks like he's home." Alex glanced at the dilapidated truck parked outside the cabin and the pack of dogs running toward them.

"Smoke from the chimney as well," Sydney pointed out.

Yvette was already greeting the dogs, slipping them treats from her pockets as she ruffled their heads. "Hey, guys. Yes, it's me again. Where's the boss?"

The boss was standing on his front porch, arms folded over his chest in a most unwelcoming posture. "What the hell are you doing here?"

"Hi, Mr. Reiner. Good to see you again too," Yvette called with utter cheerfulness.

Alex fought to keep from smiling.

Yvette gestured to the side. "This is Sydney, and I think you know Alex. He works at Silver Stone."

Creighton met Alex's gaze. "Hoity-toity horses still selling like hot cakes?"

"Yes, sir," Alex said.

"That Ashton still giving you hell?"

"Yes, sir, and he brought in his nephew as backup for the days Ashton wants to take life a little easier and sleep in."

Creighton huffed before taking in the three of them again. "You plan on giving me any kind of religious pamphlets, you can just turn yourselves right around."

Yvette had made it to the bottom rung of the stairs. "I came back to take a look at Hunter and figured while I was checking on your dog, Sydney could take a look at your foot."

"Why would I let some little girl do that?" Creighton straightened, towering over them in spite of his years.

Alex was about to remind the man of his manners when Sydney stepped forward, hands clasped in front of her as if she *were* a little girl about to make a recitation in front of the class.

She might look like a pixie, yet the next minute, Sydney proved she had balls of steel. "I graduated at the top of my class, five years younger than most men in the program. But the real reason you want me to take a look at you is because I'm also a really good shot. If I have to use a tranquilizer dart and take you down when you're out doing chores some morning and not expecting it, I will. Then I'll be real pissed I had to do that instead of starting right here and now and doing what should be a five-minute examination. Stuff your attitude and sit your ass down in a chair so I can look at those stitches. Sound like a good enough reason to you, sir?"

Alex kept an eye on Creighton but had to put a hand up to cover his mouth, pretending to scratch his cheeks, because there was no way in hell he could stop his grin.

Yvette rocked slightly, almost as if she were choking.

Sydney fluttered her lashes then switched her hands to behind her back, once again a little girl. "Shall we get on with it?"

Creighton turned on the spot and went back into the cabin, but he left the door open.

The three of them followed him in.

Yvette stopped in the doorway. "Hunter's not on the porch. You know where he's gone?"

Creighton shrugged. "Probably the barn. The dogs all got a nest out there to keep them warm in the winter."

The man leaned down to undo his boot.

Yvette tilted her head toward Sydney, indicating Alex

should stay with her, and then stepped outside, going to look for her patient.

The old man grumbled a few times, but he let Sydney examine his wound and give him a shot along with a small vial with medication. "Yvette did a good job, and it's healing well. Take the pills to make sure it stays infection free until it's completely mended."

They were headed out the door when the old man spoke gruffly. "Thanks."

"You're welcome. If you do have problems, call someone, and I'll come and check on you," Sydney promised.

"Don't push your luck," he grumbled.

Alex chuckled as they walked down the steps and headed toward the barn in search of Yvette. "That was actually very friendly for Creighton."

"He seems like a lovely gentleman," Sydney said with complete seriousness.

Yvette was in the barn, confused and worried. "I've looked everywhere, and I can't find Hunter."

Even after a joint search by all three of them, there was no sign of the dog.

She finally shrugged and pointed back toward the truck. "I'll come out again in a few days. He might've headed out to the far side of the property, and I'm not going to go wading through the snow to find him."

They dropped Sydney off first. The doctor wiggled her fingers before vanishing into her cozy little house at the edge of town.

"She's kick-ass," Yvette said happily. "I'm glad she's going to join us at the next girls' night out."

"The men in this town are not going to know what hit them," Alex complained with a shake of his head. "You ladies running wild once a month. It's just disaster waiting to happen.

Maybe you need some help at the next one. You know, some big strong guys to lift and carry things for you."

"You wish," Yvette said. "Too bad that's why we call it *girls'* night out, so you can't be invited."

"Invite me to something else, then," Alex teased.

"Maybe I will. Maybe you could come over tomorrow, and after I open my calendar surprise, you can join me when I visit my grandparents."

Alex froze, the ease with which she had asked him to do something so personal sending a thrill through him.

Before he could speak, her fingers had tightened on the wheel, and she was staring straight forward. "Never mind. That was a silly suggestion. I'm sure you have other things you need to do."

"Yvette." Her name came out sharper than intended.

She glanced at him and made a face. "Sorry."

He caught her hand in his and kissed her knuckles softly. Breathing slowly as he tried to make sure he said what she needed to hear. "I am so pleased you invited me. I'll say it again. Whatever expectations you have, we're still figuring stuff out, but I *want* to be there for you. Which means you can invite me to something, and if I can't make it, I will tell you why. And if I don't want to do it, I will tell you that as well. *Trust* me."

"I'm trying." The words escaped barely above a whisper.

He laughed, letting the sound ripple through the tightness of the space between them. "You're doing great. And I'm looking forward to seeing your grandparents, although I already know them, since Mack, Ryan, and I have been trading off doing the once-a-month fire drills at the senior lodge."

She blinked. "You're right. I'd forgotten about that." She wrinkled her nose. "Speaking of forgetting, that's the other thing. We're moving my grandpa tomorrow."

9

Ten thirty the next morning, Alex parked outside the Heart Falls Senior Lodge and hurried to join Yvette. He was running a little bit late, but she'd responded to his text with happy face emojis and an assurance she still wanted him there when he could make it.

The lodge was a cozy building, with a large central core and four residential arms. Two of those had one- or two-bedroom mini apartments for independent living. The third was for extended care, where trained healthcare workers helped with the day-to-day care of the residents.

The fourth section included an Alzheimer's and dementia ward, which is where Alex found himself headed as he helped carry the final load of Floyd Wright's possessions.

"Is it coffee time?" Yvette's grandpa asked, his voice wavering slightly as he glanced over his shoulder at his wife, who was pushing his wheelchair.

"It is," Geraldine said agreeably. "And after coffee, we'll get you settled in your new room."

"I hope they have proper cookies today." He glanced at

Yvette, who was walking beside him, a brightly coloured quilt draped over her arm. "Do you like cookies?"

"Most of the time. Especially with coffee, but I also like cinnamon rolls, and doughnuts and lots of other sweet treats."

He made an agreeable sound, nodding firmly.

Grandma Geraldine glanced at Alex, who held a banker's box in his arms. "Thank you for bringing that. We didn't have enough hands to juggle everything."

"Glad to help." They paused at the security door and waited while Yvette punched in the code.

A few minutes later, they had Floyd settled at one of the round tables in the common area. Geraldine sat beside him as the helpers brought around cups of coffee and plates of snacks.

"Here. I'll put that in Grandpa's room." Yvette reached for the box in his arms.

He chin-lifted toward the residential spaces. "You lead. I'll follow."

Yvette leaned past him to smile at her grandma. "We'll be back in a minute, Grandma."

"That's fine, sweetheart. We'll be here." She put another cookie on the plate and pushed it closer to her husband. "There. That's one of your favourites."

Floyd's new room was only a few steps away. Yvette pushed open the door and let Alex in first.

It was a simple setup with the bed along one wall and a wardrobe on the other. There was just enough room for a single reclining chair and a table pushed against the wall. A small private bathroom was the only other door in the space. But there was a large window with a deep windowsill, and a number of pretty objects were lined up there for Floyd to enjoy.

Alex placed the box on the table and reached for the quilt in Yvette's arms. "Here. I'll put that on the bed if you want to deal with the rest of what's in the box."

"I don't even know what's in the box," she confessed, but she made the trade. "I hope this goes well."

He hadn't had much chance to ask specific questions, but he knew enough about the place to understand without having been told. "I take it your grandpa needs extra help? He's not safe in the independent living section anymore?"

"No." Yvette placed another picture on the windowsill then opened drawers in the wardrobe. "My grandma will continue to live in their old apartment. She said that she'll come here to spend time with him every day. No reason why she can't do her knitting sitting here just as well."

Alex nodded as he looked around the small space and considered the cozy apartment room where he'd met them five minutes ago. "It'll work out, and I'm glad. But it's a sad stage of life in some ways."

He straightened from smoothing the quilt to find Yvette with her arms folded over her chest and sadness in her eyes.

Her head tilted. "Can I get a hug?"

"Of course, sweetheart." He wrapped her up, pressing a kiss to her forehead before easing her head against his neck. "They're good people, and this is a good place. You don't have to worry about them."

"I'm not," Yvette insisted quietly. "It's just..."

She squeezed him tight as she took a breath in and let it out slowly.

Alex stood and held her. Let her think and let her feel. "We can talk about this more later if you want. I've a feeling if we don't get out there soon, though, your grandfather's going to eat every one of the cookies at the table."

A small laugh escaped. "You're right."

She eased back far enough to kiss him softly then caught him by the fingers and pulled him back into the common room.

Grandma Geraldine was chatting with a woman on her left. Grandpa Floyd appeared to have finished his coffee and his cookies and was now relaxing in his chair, head nodding slightly.

Alex settled to his right, Yvette beside him. Yvette joined in the conversation with the ladies.

Alex listened without interrupting, looking around at the workers and residents and quietly being there while Geraldine began this new part of her life and a new stage with her life partner.

He'd meant it when he told Yvette that the lodge was a good place. He wasn't worried at all about Floyd—he'd be well cared for. Well loved.

Only, it was a change. More so than anything Alex had ever had to face...

Which brought up memories from his past. Hell, every part of life, every season had challenges. Had good and bad, but both of those were better to face with someone who truly cared.

For Floyd, that was Geraldine. Plus Yvette, and if Alex was truly going to be a part of her world, that meant that this elderly couple sitting nearby needed to be a part of his world as well.

It was an inspiring moment that hit deep inside him.

The ladies were still talking. Looking for distraction, he discovered a rolling tray set against the wall behind them, and he pulled it over to examine a partially begun game of checkers. He examined the board, trying to figure out the best next move.

He glanced up to discover Floyd watching him intently.

One shaking finger slowly extended over the edge of the wheelchair and nudged a checker to a new position. Then Floyd leaned back and pretended to be asleep.

Oh. It was going to be like that, was it? Alex glanced at the ladies, but none of them were paying any attention. He grinned at Floyd and silently moved his own piece.

Alex waited. It took a little bit before one eye peeked open.

The next instant, Floyd's face lit up with an enormous grin before the smile vanished. Intently, he leaned forward, reaching over the game—

He picked up one of his men and triple jumped Alex's pieces, wiping out half of the men he had remaining.

Alex blinked. *The hell?*

He glanced at Floyd then bit back a chuckle of amusement. Because the old man was once again easing into the cushions on his chair, eyes closed. A soft snore rumbled as if he was asleep. Whether it was fake or real, the man had killer timing.

Alex was still chuckling as he and Yvette took their leave.

She paused beside her truck, looking thoughtful. "You still want to come over?"

"Definitely. You need to open day twelve."

It was a warm enough day that Alex settled in the Adirondack chair and groaned as he stretched his legs out. "That feels good. Just let me relax for a minute or two."

Yvette chuckled as she tossed him a quilt then settled in the chair beside him. "Rough night?"

"Maybe I'm just getting old," Alex confessed. "Staying up late or getting up early aren't the problem. It's the staying up late *and* getting up early I'm finding a little less entertaining."

Her gaze met his, and a sweet smile crossed her face. "Thank you so much for coming with me today. It meant a lot."

"I was glad to do it." The words came easy. Now Alex wondered about the other revelation that had come to him.

Before he could say anything, though, Yvette spoke up. "How are your parents doing?"

"Good. Really good." Especially after Davis had contacted him with a full update on everything he was taking care of. It seemed leopards could change their spots. "I think there are still moments that Dad overdoes it, but that's kind of par for the course with him."

"It's really nice that you went out there to take care of

them." She made a face and paused. She seemed to be struggling to find words. A soft shrug lifted her shoulders. "You have a really great relationship with them."

"They haven't always been perfect, but they've always tried." She didn't seem in a hurry to get on with opening up her Advent calendar, and Alex had nowhere he needed to be for a while. A chance to talk seem long overdue. "They pretty much saved my life."

Her eyes were full of wonder. Seriousness there, and concern. "You were a foster kid, right?"

He nodded. "My mom wasn't the best. My birth mom, that is. She shouldn't have been a mom in the first place, so I don't really think any less of her. When she gave me up, getting placed with the Thorne family set me on a whole different path than I would've travelled otherwise."

Yvette nodded slowly. "I'm glad. They sound like neat people."

"They're my family. I officially took their last name as mine when I turned eighteen because I wanted to make that point." To Alex, that said all that needed to be said. Only, she still seemed to have something on her mind, which he could completely understand. "Are you worried about your grandparents?"

"My grandma, a little," she confessed. "Really, at this point, my grandpa doesn't remember enough to be upset long-term over anything. Plus, being around trained caregivers will help a whole lot more in those moments when he does react badly. My grandma couldn't keep dealing with sundowner's syndrome and physically caring for him."

"Your grandmother knows you're here. She seems the type who will ask for help if she needs it," Alex reassured her.

She nodded. A small motion, but firm. "I'm very glad I came out to Heart Falls when I did." She met his gaze straight on and steady. "I got to have time with my grandpa before he got too forgetful. I regret all the years we didn't have together."

"Why did you not have them in your life?" The words escaped before he realized it might be a little too personal. A little too sensitive, then the thought that he wanted *all* of her returned. Not just her joys but her sorrows.

He wanted to be there, to be there for her, which meant he needed to know what was wrong and what was right and what sorrows he needed to share to lighten her burden.

Yvette stared at her hands. "My parents cut ties with my grandparents over fifteen years ago. Closer to twenty. I'm not exactly sure, because we didn't live that close, so in some ways it made sense. Us kids noticed when Christmas presents didn't arrive. And birthday presents, and no more phone calls."

That bit of information shocked Alex.

"Your grandparents stopped trying to get in touch with you?" All sorts of terrible things rushed into his mind. "What happened? Why did your parents do that?"

Yvette took a big breath, curling the quilt tighter around her shoulders before she met his gaze firmly. "My mom insisted that they were doing what was best for our family. That we needed to be together and one unit, unified. That spending time with Grandma and Grandpa was not a part of being a healthy family."

Jeez. Alex had friends who had cut ties with their parents. Sometimes it was because of blatantly terrible stuff, like sexual abuse or neglect. Recently, a lot more were situations where it simply was in a person's best interest to no longer listen to voices of people who had priorities vastly different than the new path they were trying to walk.

Only, that didn't explain why Yvette had come to Heart Falls to renew the relationship with the people who had been cut off...

Oh.

He examined her closely. "I'm guessing that at some point you decided your parents' decision to cut ties wasn't *really* in your best interest."

"I think the estrangement was more that my grandma and grandpa didn't approve of the way my mom and dad acted. It caused less guilt to not have the voice of reason hanging over their heads."

Alex sat forward in his seat. "Are you okay?"

She wrinkled her nose, thinking hard. "I am. Honestly. There are just certain moments when, as an adult, it hits really hard that some of the people who *should* care for us *don't*. Yet, a lot of people who, when there's no reason why they need to care, do. I'm working through that."

They were too damn far apart for this type of conversation. Alex patted his lap and opened his arms. "That's the part about being an adult that both sucks and is wonderful. But you don't have to work through it over there, all alone."

She shook her head even as she dropped the quilt and crossed to his side. Then she was curled up in his lap with her head against his shoulder. "Thank you again for coming with me today. I know it meant a lot to my grandma. She's who I want to focus on now."

With Yvette in his arms, her warmth resting against his chest, Alex breathed in deep and soaked in the pleasure of her trust. Because that's what it was, having her there after what she'd just confessed.

"It was my pleasure." A thought occurred to him. A wicked, wonderful thought. "Cuddle in for a bit, but then it's time for you to open the next day of your calendar."

SOMETHING INSIDE HER ACHED, but strangely, contentment grew as well. The old pain wasn't wrapped up in a tangle of barbed wire, sharp edges cutting into her every time she moved.

Her family had hurt her. Still hurt her, if she were being honest.

It was an injury, and it was still there but as if the wound had been washed clean and begun to heal.

Forget pretending that it had never existed—being able to honestly say she could move forward was a dream Yvette hadn't dared to dream yet.

She caught herself stroking the neckline of Alex's coat, his skin hot under her fingers. The time they'd spent sitting together over the past couple weeks, sometimes necking, sometimes just lazily touching each other, made it too easy to consider giving in to the rising heat.

But first, something precious needed to be recognized. She slid her hand up to his cheek, lifting her chin until their eyes met. "I'm enjoying my present," she admitted. "You're very creative."

He kissed her. Once. A small, soft press of their lips together. Just enough to set a flutter going in her heart.

"Good inspiration," he teased. "Want to go get your key?"

Her legs were shaky. When Alex planted a hand on her butt to help her balance, copping a feel at the same time, the zing of lightning up her spine helped her to dance away, glancing back at him. "Handsy."

"Any time. Anywhere," he promised.

She laughed all the way to where the key hung waiting for her.

Alex stood beside the desk as she slid the key in and opened the small drawer in the back of the writing desk to reveal—

"A deck of cards?" She raised a brow. "Um, thank you?"

"Ha. That's not just any deck of cards."

She eyed him up and down, taking her time and enjoying the view. "A special deck made for strip poker?"

He grinned. "Not hardly. We're nowhere near that stage."

Disappointment shouldn't have been the biggest thing to hit. "Okay, then. What's the game? And the stakes?"

He caught her by the hand and led her into the cabin, pulling off his coat and boots and making his way to the table to shuffle the deck. "Questions and kisses."

Well, she could get on board with part of his suggestion. "You're a pretty good kisser. I suppose I can agree to that. But what does the question part mean?"

His grin only got wider. "I propose we play war. Best of three hands. Winner gets to ask a question; loser has to kiss the winner."

He was a turkey. "That doesn't sound as if anybody loses."

"Nope. It's a fast way to get to know more about each other, but I also really want to kiss you." The heat in his eyes was enough to ignite her on the spot.

"But only the loser gets to kiss," she reminded him.

"I'm a shitty cardplayer."

She laughed, grabbing them both glasses of water before settling kitty-corner at the table. She took the half deck he proffered and placed it squarely in front of her. "Prepare yourself."

His eyes flashed.

First card flip, she had a ten, he had a five. She slid the cards to her side of the table and snapped up the next card. A four, which he beat easily.

"Tiebreaker, for the first round of rewards. Go," Alex said.

They both revealed their cards, and he beat her by one, eight to a seven.

Only, considering the way he'd set up the game, she didn't think it was much of a loss. "What's your question?"

Alex eased back in his chair and folded his arms over his

chest. His gaze drifted over her. Slowly, a teasing caress. Her nipples hardened, and her heart rate increased, just from the man being a cocky bastard.

It wasn't fair.

Chances were, he would ask something totally embarrassing, and the heat in her cheeks would continue to rise.

"If you were going to take a vacation, would you pick a beach, a lake, or mountain cabin? Or something entirely different?"

Well, now. That was unexpected.

Yvette paused to consider. "If it's vacation where I want to relax, I have to go with the mountain cabin. If it's for adventure, I'd pick either the beach or somewhere with a lot of history. Museums, big churches. That sort of thing. Although I've never really done a lot of travel."

His expression changed. "Huh. That's a good point. The relaxing versus adventure part."

He reached for the cards, but Yvette clicked her tongue in warning. "Hold your horses, buster. My turn."

Which is when she discovered a logistical error. Kissing him with the corner of a table between them was nowhere near the experience she was looking for. Not today.

"Come on." She grabbed her cards, indicated he should do the same, then caught him by the hand and guided him into her bedroom.

He didn't say anything. Just obediently sat on the spot she patted, his grin firmly in place. "You're absolutely right. I'll win even when I lose."

"You were too far away from me before," she explained primly.

Yvette leaned forward. Alex met her in the middle. She pressed a palm to his cheek and stared at his face before kissing him. Slow, steamy, but very much with her in control, because when she moved back, he stayed there. Eyes closed, grin spreading like honey on warm toast.

"I am so liking this game." He all but purred it, dark eyes smoldering.

She nudged him with an elbow, hiding a smile. "Get your cards ready."

He grabbed his stash but also wiggled back on the bed, sprawling comfortably. She sat cross-legged, placing her first card down.

A king. Alex laid down a two.

"Crap, that was a waste of a good card," Yvette complained.

Her second card and her third were beat by his.

Once again, he looked her over steadily. Heat rising in his eyes as he considered his question. "What's the one thing you want me to know about your body?"

She stalled. "Like, what?"

He was up on one elbow, cards pushed aside. He trailed his fingers up her arm until his heated thumb teased along her neckline. "What do you like in bed, Yvette? Slow buildup? Hard and fast? A little of both?"

Sex. After all the fooling around they'd been doing, putting sex on the table was the question.

Did she want it? Definitely.

His thumb rested at the base of her throat, teasing back and forth. She pulled her scattered brains together. "I don't think I can tell you one thing. I don't—"

She paused again, deliberately this time. He'd asked her to trust him in so many ways; this was a huge area where she would *also* demand trust. She deserved it. Deserved to be able to say what she wanted.

"I want exclusivity. I want time to get to know what we like. I don't want a checklist or round-the-bases momentum. I want what feels good for both of us."

Before he could move, she did. Pushing against his chest so

he was flat on his back on her bed. One more adjustment, and she was straddling him, hips resting over his solid thighs.

The heat in his eyes flashed brighter.

Yvette ran her fingers up the placket of his shirt. "You didn't specify where I was allowed to kiss. You want to?"

"Anywhere. Everywhere." The words came out one step above a growl.

She slipped his first button. His second. Leaning forward as she continued to undo his shirt. She pushed aside the layers of fabric to expose his firm chest with the faint trace of dark hair.

His chest rose and fell with his rapid breaths.

She placed her hands on him. Heat scalded her palms. Using him as a base, she leveraged up high enough to be able to meet his gaze straight on for a split second before dropping her eyes to his lips. Kissing their strong surface. Moving to his chin and down his neck. The taste of him stealing in as she briefly stroked her tongue against his skin. The scent of clean soap and masculine musk filled her senses.

She kissed her way down his body, stopping inches above his belly button. The ridges of his abdomen were like rocks, and she traced them with her fingers before following with her mouth.

The sounds escaping him made her entire body tense. The thick length of his erection was clearly visible under his jeans as she slid between his legs.

A second later, she blinked in shock as her deck of cards appeared in front of her, right there on top of his belly. He curled up far enough, she scrambled to grab them before they flew everywhere.

"Deal your cards," he growled, slapping his on the bed beside them. A five. Which she easily beat with the ten she flipped over.

Her second card was a three, and she figured they were

going to need to go to a third to break the tie when he slapped a deuce on top of it. "You win," he declared.

An instant later she was lying on her back with him perched over her. Thighs nestled between hers, his heavy weight sealing their lower torsos together.

He braced his elbows on either side of her head. "What's your question?"

She had to think of something to ask him? Good grief, how was she expected to think right now?

"Later. Kiss me," she demanded.

His grin flared as he tossed her earlier words back at him. "You never specified where I'm allowed to kiss you."

"Anywhere. Everywhere," she begged.

"Good answer."

He took her lips. Nothing controlled or contained, especially not with the weight of him resting so perfectly over her. When he stroked his tongue against her lips, she opened with a moan, tangling her fingers in his hair to keep him right there. He slid his tongue languidly in and out, rolling his hips at the same time, the same speed. Teasing his hardness against her sensitive core.

He broke away, caught hold of the bottom of her T-shirt, and peeled it off her body. Then the kisses resumed. A series along her collarbone, a teasing nip along the edge of her bra. He cupped one hand over her breast then circled his cheek against her other nipple. The tight tip tingled with every brush of his five o'clock scruff.

Yvette closed her eyes and let the warmth of his mouth going down her body ignite every nerve. Every wonderful bit in her that knew there was nothing wrong in this moment. She didn't want for anything, except more of what he was giving.

When he finally undid the button on her jeans, dragging down the zipper so slowly, each tooth that released rasped in her ears like a gunshot, she took an unsteady breath in.

He caught both her jeans and panties at the same time and stripped them away.

It took every bit of courage to keep her lips pressed together. To not say something like *oh, you don't have to do that.* To say it was her turn to give to him.

A needy groan escaped him, and she adjusted up onto her elbows to take in the scene. To truly appreciate the sight of the handsome man between her thighs, staring at her sex with hunger written all over him.

He shook his head. "I have wanted this for so long."

Still watching, which Yvette wasn't sure if that made the anticipation better or worse, she felt a quiver ripple over her skin. He moved so slowly, inching his way toward where she needed him most.

He trailed his fingers from her belly button to the top of her mound, cupping her firmly before sliding his fingers into her curls and opening her.

With a deep breath, he leaned in and kissed her. One perfect, gentle kiss.

Then he turned ravenous, his tongue conquering, fingers taking. His free arm pinned her to the bed as he licked and sucked, pumping his fingers into her sex and driving her wild with need.

It was wild and fast, and it was perfect.

If she'd had to describe what she wanted, this wouldn't have been it, but now that he was here, doing what he wanted, giving to her, nothing else could've been better.

"God, you taste good." He stroked his fingers inside her again then renewed his assault on her clit.

Yvette's knees fell apart, and she buried her fingers in his hair, hips undulating against him as heat rose. As she reached inside for release.

He gave it to her. Just the right tease, just the right pressure. When he closed his lips over her clit and sucked in time with the pulse of his fingers, she nearly flew off the bed. "*Alex.*"

Without pausing his hand, he lifted and came down against her side. Hips rocking hard, his cock an iron brand against her thigh as he stole her breath with a wicked kiss. His touch demanded she accept every last pulse of the orgasm controlling her core.

It took a while to come back down, especially with his lips on hers. He eased his fingers out slowly, pausing to tease. To nip at her bottom lip. To stroke his thumb over her clit.

Every single action caused her body to roll with lingering pleasure.

She slid her fingers through his hair. His pleased grin was visible for a second before he wiped his mouth with the back of his hand.

"Told you I'd win."

Yvette fluttered her lashes at him. "We're not done yet."

His lips twitched, then he coughed. "We most definitely are."

Wait. *What*?

She reached down, but before she made contact with his abdomen, he caught her wrists and pinned them to the bed beside her body. A subtle change in his expression caught her attention and...

"Are you *blushing*?"

His grin widened, but his cheeks were most definitely rosier than before. "You make the most delicious noises when you come, Yvette Wright. Way to knock me off my game."

Shock and something that felt a little like pride snuck in. To learn he'd been so turned on by their fooling around that he came just rubbing on her sent heat rushing all over again.

Still, she wasn't sure what was appropriate at a moment like this. "If you're saying what I think you're saying, do I apologize or congratulate you?"

"Life happens. Just don't laugh." He rolled back to the mattress, his expression sheepish. "Although maybe we should laugh together. Holy *hell*, woman. I haven't lost control like that in... Well, I don't remember when."

"I'm sure blocking that sort of memory is a good, healthy choice that all guys do on a regular basis."

This time, Alex snickered. "You're probably right. Though it's not really a topic of conversation with my friends. At least not since we got out of grade school."

"Go on," Yvette teased. "I'm pretty sure that dirty talk about everything from sex to masturbation gets airtime during your firefighting shifts."

"True. But you think any of us want to confess we've got the staying power of a teenager?" He kissed her again. Slow and deep and wet and delicious. Pulling his lips from hers barely far enough so that when he spoke, warm air teased past her cheek. "I'm happy. That's enough for now. Let me hold you for a bit."

She curled her arms around him. Not trying to push them farther or faster, but enjoying the deep connection between them, right then, right there.

Alex pressed one final kiss to the tip of her nose then tucked her head under his chin. Yvette breathed out a happy sigh. Warm, sated.

Amusement still tickled inside her at his awkward condition, but even that was right. The level of trust that made it possible to simply soak in this moment and deal with *life happens* later—it was powerful.

She leaned harder into his embrace and enjoyed the giddy sensations spilling through her soul.

10

Daydreaming, Yvette all but floated her way out onto the porch with her day-fourteen key, ready to find out what sweet thing Alex had put in today's drawer to make her smile.

Today made two weeks, and Yvette wondered at how much things had changed.

Oh, she still understood why past Alex had gotten on her nerves. But he'd changed, a lot, since those days. While he still managed to say things that got her back up, it was usually because she'd planned on being offended in the first place. She had her hot buttons, that much was clear.

But now *she* was trying to change as well.

She glanced again at the key chain, this one a tiny candle. Both the key chain and the key were delicate, and she thought she knew which cubbyhole on the dresser it would open. One of the ones hidden behind the writer's desk rolltop.

Even though she was sure, she hadn't even looked for the drawer until now. Not even tempted to be honest. The waiting time was turning out to be a delicious sort of anticipation. Something she'd never known she would like so very much.

Kind of how taking things forward sexually had been delayed, and even though they were still not all the way there, one step at a time was working out perfectly. Eventually, they'd have sex. Wicked, wild, dirty, hot...

Maybe because she was distracted by sex thoughts, she shoved the rolltop up a little too quickly. The key chain slipped from her hand, skidding across the smooth wooden surface of the desk.

Yvette watched, horrified, as the key and key chain vanished from sight, slipping down a narrow crack between the desktop and the side panel.

The string of curses escaping her lips were both loud and inventive but far too heartfelt to be admired. "What have I done?"

She banged on the side of the chest, peering down the crack then flopping onto the ground to see if by some miracle the board was warped all the way from top to bottom and the key had fallen through. No such luck.

She hurried into the house and grabbed a hammer and screwdriver, not even sure at that point what she was going to do. If she couldn't find the key, everything was at a standstill. All of Alex's hard work, ruined.

Even with the flashlight, and carefully feeding a bent coat hanger into the crack, she came up empty.

Yvette examined the side closer then tugged the bureau forward. Relief swept in. The back was held on by a series of screws. If she took it off, she might be able to loosen the side panel enough to release her key. She went to work, carefully putting each screw in a bowl.

She was halfway down when the chest creaked, the sound of wood sliding on wood. Excited, she put a hand on the back and on the side and carefully tugged—

Something metallic clattered to the porch, landing with a distinctive *ping*.

She crawled out from her awkward position, got on her knees, sweeping a hand underneath and dragging forward—

Oh my God.

She blinked, but it didn't change anything. On the ground before her was the key chain she'd been looking for. But something else sparkled up at her. Her heart raced, and her mouth went dry as she picked it up.

It was a ring. Silver, or maybe white gold, with two little diamond chips on either side of a pink stone. It was pretty, it was perfect. It appealed to every bit of her magpie, trinket-loving soul.

But *oh my God*. It was a *ring*.

What the hell?

Yes, she'd committed to this crazy dating thing, and so far, it was going okay.

Liar. It was going spectacularly.

But a *ring*? That was presumptuous. Preposterous. No way. What was Alex thinking?

I could easily fall in love with you.

He'd admitted as much right off the bat. And when people were in love, they did things like get married.

Nope. Her mind could not handle this. It was way beyond comprehension.

She collapsed into one of the chairs beside the bureau and sat in utter confusion.

What did she do now?

"I REALLY THINK it's the best plan." Tucker Stewart paced forward at his usual breakneck speed. The one that made Alex move double time to keep up.

"I agree. No need to keep extra stock if we're not going to

use them. But there's plenty of room for the kids to take over that part of the care. Chores do a person good." Alex snickered. "Dear God, I should get you to record me saying that so I can send it to my dad. He'll get a good laugh out of it."

The other man grinned. "Always a jolt to the system when I hear my uncle's words coming out of my mouth. As long as it's the good stuff, it's not so bad. Hate it when it's the stuff that drove me crazy because he was *wrong*."

"That would be too nice. We both know it doesn't work that way," Alex drawled. "Holy hell."

They both jerked to a stop. They'd rounded the corner outside the barn and ran smack into a herd of goats. Not a trio of goats, aka the hellions that actually belong to Silver Stone ranch. No, these were most definitely brand-new beasts and rather put out with being tied in place. The old billy shook his head menacingly, while the dam bleated, loud and long. The pair of kids at her heels took up the cry, and it was one step short of bedlam, especially when the goats at the other end of the yard joined in the chorus.

"Christ, is this like socks multiplying in the dryer?" Tucker glanced around. "How did they get here?"

No one in the yard could answer that question. There were no trucks around that weren't supposed to be there, either.

Alex did the next thing. He clicked his tongue, moving closer to the animals. "Well, they can't stay here. You want me to put them in with the pets or stick them in a separate pen while we ask around?"

Tucker joined him, soothing the beasts. Taking a quick look at their eyes and in their mouths. "They look fit enough, but until we get a clean bill of health, we're not putting them in with our animals. Use the pen across from Eeny, Meany, and Miney. Once these new ones are checked by the vet, we'll decide what to do with them."

Alex untied the ropes and guided the mini herd to their new pen, gears turning in his head. He could've sworn he'd seen these animals recently. Of course, it wasn't until he penned them up that he realized where that was.

Creighton Reiner's.

Alex didn't want to say anything until he was certain, which meant at the end of his workday, he found himself taking the strange road up to the old man's ranch.

The entire way there, he had a whole new set of questions buzzing in his brain. Like why the hell the man had built his road this direction? Straight as an arrow, true. But it certainly wasn't the shortest access route from Heart Falls.

In the yard at Reiner's, Alex stopped and listened hard. Smoke rose from the chimney, but the man's beat-up old truck was nowhere to be seen.

On the off chance there was another reason for the missing truck, Alex decided to explore anyway. The dogs came to greet him as usual, the pack of them jumping and barking and altogether excited in the typical way of farm dogs.

Alex tossed them treats then walked with an escort up to the cabin. Banging loudly, he gave a shout. "Creighton. You've got a visitor."

No one answered. A quick peek inside proved the cabin was empty. It only took ten minutes to walk through the small outbuildings, with no sign of the owner.

Also, no sign of the goats Alex had seen on his previous visit.

In fact, there were a whole lot of animals missing. The barn held only Creighton's horse and a single milk cow, both old enough that they should've been retired years ago.

"What the hell are you up to, old man?" Alex muttered.

He took a final swing around the far side of the outbuildings. The farm was a little disorganized, but it had good bones. Creighton also had the biggest stock of firewood Alex had ever seen, and that part was meticulously lined up and layered to dry. He probably had the next two years' supply prepared.

A stack of logs blocked the main trail, so Alex stepped into the nearby bushes to get around them.

He stopped in his tracks, distracted by a pile of newly disturbed dirt. A moment's closer examination proved it was a newly dug grave. A simple board pounded into the softer earth with shaky handwriting on the cross piece that stated *Hunter*.

Well, damn. It seemed the old-timer's beast hadn't made it after all. Yvette was going to be disappointed, even though she knew it was the way of the world.

Alex said a final farewell to the enthusiastic trio still guarding the farm then made his way back to his truck and down the long road. Back toward his place at the bunkhouse. He'd track down Creighton another day.

He wasn't about to share the bad news with Yvette tonight. Not when she had time with her girls to enjoy.

So he did what he'd always do in this circumstance. Headed for the fire hall. A chance to chat with good people, shoot the breeze, and get out of his own head.

A way to resist the urge to sneak into Yvette's party, even if it were just to steal a kiss.

"There are strange things afoot in Heart Falls." This pronouncement came from Tansy as she placed two pitchers on the table in front of Yvette. "Purple one is the sangria—thank you to Alex for the fixings—and the pink is lemonade, for those of you not imbibing."

"Alex bought our drinks?" Hanna looked confused.

"It was in my Advent calendar dating gift chest," Yvette said before turning to Brooke. "Can we please come up with some shorter code name for whatever this is I'm doing with Alex?"

"That begs the question. What *are* you doing with him?" Rose waggled her brows, and a snicker rose from the gathered group.

Yvette's cheeks flushed. "No comment."

Tansy grabbed a glass and poured it full of the sangria, settling on the couch. "Ignore the fact that Rose and Alex dated for a while. Because it's totally ignorable."

"We just went dancing a bunch of times. Really. There wasn't anything more," Rose insisted. "He's a nice guy, but there were no sparks."

"Do you even have a spark detector?" Tansy teased.

"Shut. Up," Rose said, turning back to Yvette. "Just in case I didn't make it clear, I think he's a great guy, and I'm really happy that you two are a couple. He deserves somebody nice."

Brooke had poured herself a glass of lemonade and settled on the couch beside Tansy. "Only in a small town would we need to have this kind of conversation."

"Dating pools. So damn shallow," Tansy complained.

The newcomer at the table for this girls' night out glanced around the room as if putting names with faces. Sydney Jeremiah grabbed her wineglass and held it toward the lemonade. "I will take the alcohol-free choice, not because I'm breeding, but because I'm on shift early tomorrow. Dealing with sick people with cranky attitudes is something that's much better while not hungover."

"I'm glad you could join us," Brooke said sincerely. "When Yvette suggested you, it made total sense."

"Yes, because we need to keep replacing all the ladies who can't join us because they're up to their eyeballs in kids."

"Hey. I'm still here," Hanna said.

"So am I," Madison added, although she didn't move from the easy chair where she'd settled, hand resting on the swell of her belly.

Yvette eyed Brooke and then the others in attendance. "Oh, we know that the Heart Falls girls' night out gatherings are always open to alumni. We're pleased there are new distractions occupying their time. The revolving door means we all get plenty of time to visit when it works out."

"Except I'm a lifetime attendee," Tansy insisted. "I will be the last woman standing. Solo, that is."

Hanna snickered, the sound somewhat out of place from the quiet woman's typical response. She glanced at Sydney. "Tansy has not yet learned the rule that it's dangerous to poke fate."

"Hey, I have my own home, I have my own business, and I like to cook more than I like to eat out. One of my best friends is a mechanic. I have no need for a man." Tansy wrinkled her nose. "Okay, except for one thing. But I can borrow guys for short periods of time for that when necessary."

Her sister Rose gasped before smacking her lightly. "*Tansy.*"

"What?" Tansy pulled on a confused and innocent expression before rolling her eyes. "Not for sex. *Jeez.* I meant for dancing. You have such a dirty mind."

The laughter continued as the girls all settled into positions around Tansy and Rose's living space. The small apartment over Buns and Roses was snug and comfortable, and Yvette made herself let go at least temporarily of the discomfort she'd been carrying since her discovery of the ring that morning.

She still wasn't sure what to do, but since there were still ten days to Christmas, it wasn't a problem she needed solved right now.

When she caught Rose examining her, Yvette offered a wink. She'd known the dark-haired beauty had gone out with

Alex before, and she'd always wondered what had happened. It was good to hear there were no lingering feelings. Yvette liked spending time with the ladies, including Rose. She didn't want to give up any of her friends.

On her right, Sydney stretched her legs out. "This is cozy," she said quietly to Yvette.

"They're a good group. It's always nice to have downtime with people who want the best for you."

Sydney dipped her chin. "I need more of that in my life. Looking forward to a little less work and a little more enjoying time with friends."

"You can afford to do that, even while starting up your own clinic?"

"It'll take some schedule juggling and being firm with myself about not taking on too much. But, yes, I think it's time." Sydney examined Yvette. "Besides, the dating pool is shallow, so there's no way I can actually get my feet wet if I spend all my time working."

"True." It seemed to Yvette that had to be the only reason Sydney wasn't already all tied up by someone special. The woman was beautiful, smart, and cocky as hell. She oozed confidence. "So, looking for love?"

Sydney snickered. "Not so much looking as no longer avoiding. What I need is for someone to fall into my lap kind of like you and Alex. I can't believe that the two of you have been officially going out for less than a month."

Fourteen days. Yvette's brain ping-ponged between how good the time with Alex had been and the discovery of that damn ring. "We annoyed each other for at least two years first."

It seemed to be the safest thing to discuss.

There was no ring—push it away. Don't think about it right now.

Fortunately, Sydney was contemplating her drink rather than watching Yvette fidget. "I mean it. The two of you fit together as if you've been dating for ages. And it's not like those people who gush over how everything is always so wonderful between them and their partner. You guys are real. Like, there's momentary tensions, but there's also this neat connection. As if you could have a shouting match but still be solid at the end of it."

Yvette stared dumbfounded for a minute before finding her voice. "Well, that's a very nice compliment."

"I don't hand out bullshit," Sydney said dryly. "Take it or leave it, that's what I see."

Their conversation was interrupted by Tansy clinking a fork on the edge of a pile of plates. She placed them onto the table then hurried back with an amazing-smelling chocolate cake.

"Food. Now I need to tell you what I wanted to tell you at the start." She mock glared at Rose. "I'm pretty sure you're the one who distracted me.

"I'm sure even if I weren't, you'd find some way to blame me," Rose said with the long-suffering ease of a sister.

"*Anyway.*" Tansy served up an enormous piece of cake to Yvette. "I was driving by the animal shelter, and there was this truck parked off to the side. The next thing I hear, Sonora has discovered three cows inside the arena."

"Not your typical rescue animal," Brooke offered sagely.

"One hundred percent true." Tansy raised her glass in the air.

Yvette was confused. "So, who dropped them off?"

Tansy wrinkled her nose. "I don't know."

"But you saw someone parked there."

"I did. A white truck."

Brooke and Yvette exchanged exasperated glances before turning back to Tansy. "Really? You didn't recognize the vehicle?"

"God, you guys, you've got the wrong woman. Yvette can tell who's driving toward her by recognizing the shade and shape of their headlights. Brooke knows the rumble of everyone's engine. Whereas Tansy recognizes her own vehicle by hitting the alarm on her key ring and following the sound." Rose ducked away before Tansy could hit her. "The truth hurts, sis."

"You're no better," Tansy retorted.

Rose straightened. "I drive a blue 2016 Hyundai."

Tansy made a rude noise. "You memorized that right before coming in. What's your license number?"

"Guys." Yvette leaned back in her chair, laughing at them. "Back to the point—a white truck doesn't narrow it down very much. Not in rural Alberta."

Madison made a noise, and the entire room instantly pivoted their attention to her.

She glared at all of them. "Stop that."

"Stop what?" Brooke asked cheerfully. "You need something, darlin'?"

"I hate you," Madison grumbled before extending a hand. "Hoist me up. I need the bathroom, and this evil chair of Tansy's is trying to swallow me whole."

"It is rather soft and people-swallowing," Tansy admitted. She and Brooke both helped Madison find her feet. "I'll set up a different chair for once you're back."

Madison grinned. "Good. Make it one close to another plate of chocolate cake, and I'll name the baby after you."

"Don't make promises you can't keep," Tansy warned.

"It's really good cake," Madison said cheerfully. "I'm sure Ryan would understand."

The rest of the evening was sweet and comfortable, and the time spent with her girlfriends filled a place inside Yvette that desperately needed it.

Holiday music played in the background, and every now and then, one or another of them would start singing along and then the group would join in, belting out the words together. Happy songs, sad ones.

Rose pulled Yvette to her feet when "Please Come Home for Christmas" came on. A deep, rumbling version that set the group laughing as Rose reached for the low notes instead of shifting to a higher key.

But it was the Carrie Underwood and John Legend version of "Hallelujah" that set Yvette's heart whirling. So much meaning, so much fierce joy and yearning in the words. Especially when harmonized by the group of women surrounding her.

Let the lonely know their worth.

Yvette's loneliness was fading. The friends in this room, the companionship of good co-workers.

Alex's company.

She still might not know what to do about the ring she'd found, but there were other parts of knowing her worth that she needed to claim. She needed to find joy in the changes.

She fell asleep that night dreaming she sang with a choir of angels, a familiar male voice beside her, and no sorrow or unhappiness could possibly touch her.

The next day, Yvette was sitting in her truck, grabbing some lunch, as a text came in.

Alex: *Morning, sweetheart*
Yvette: *Nearly afternoon. Had a busy day?*
Alex: *Out of cell phone range and headed there again. Wanted to know how your day was going.*

She considered, focusing on the good bits she'd been dreaming about and not the fact she'd found a ring the previous day.

Ignoring *that* seemed the smartest thing for now.

Yvette: *Three emergencies at the clinic and a horse out at Greenfields. But all turned out well.*

Alex: Of course. They had you taking care of them.

He was too sweet. Yvette put through a call.

"Hey," he answered with a smile in his voice. "I've got maybe five minutes before I lose reception. Tucker's driving."

"No problem. Just wanted to say thank you for the sangria. The girls appreciated it."

"Glad it was good." He lowered his voice. "I miss you."

It had been only a couple days since they'd been together, but she had to admit the truth. "I miss you too."

"Tell me something fun," he ordered.

"There were rescue cows at Sonora's. Someone else says they found three extra rabbits in their hutch this morning. And Meyer's had extra chickens."

"Huh." He paused. "We had goats dumped on us at Silver Stone. I went looking. I think they're Creighton's animals."

"That's what I thought, too."

"Yvette? Bad news. I went up to his place after we found the goats. Didn't see Creighton, but Hunter passed away."

"Oh." Sadness hit, but she took a deep breath and pushed past it. "He wasn't in any pain. I figured it would happen eventually. I hope Creighton's all right."

"Me too," Alex said. "Hey, need to run, but if you want, I can take you up to Creighton's tomorrow or the next day. Just to check things out. Let me know."

"Okay. I'll think about it."

"Later, sweetheart."

He was gone before she answered.

She leaned back and considered. The call with Alex? Totally sweet.

The situation with Creighton and the animals? Wildly curious. What was going on?

Minding her own business didn't seem right. Not at all.

Which meant the next chance she got to visit a certain elderly farmer, she was going to take it.

That chance came only a few hours later when she finished her workday early.

She hoped one cranky farmer was prepared to spill his secrets.

11

They hadn't had any fresh snow in the past week, but the temperatures had stayed cold enough that the muddy ruts in the road up to Creighton's had frozen rock solid. Yvette's truck vibrated as she drove the worst washboard she'd experienced in a long time.

Still, her curiosity was high enough that something needed to be done. While Alex had offered to go with her, she didn't want to wait. She figured she had the excuse of coming for an uninvited visit as Creighton's veterinarian.

The fact that Hunter was gone made her sad, but the dog had been old. Maybe with a little extra TLC, he could've lived on until the spring, maybe through the summer. But there were no guarantees about that, and she definitely didn't want Creighton thinking she was upset at him.

Ranching was full of choices, and sometimes what seemed wrong to a person made more sense after a little conversation. That talk time is what she wanted to offer the man.

She parked next to his old beater, curiosity making her steal a peek into the truck bed. Stray bits of straw were not so much of a clue as a simple fact of life in the country.

The farm dogs appeared briefly before returning to wherever they were hiding from the cold as she made her way to the little cabin. She knocked, then stuck her gloved hands under her armpits to keep warm.

Creighton pulled the door open all of an inch before glaring at her with one eye. "What?"

"Can I come in?"

"Why?"

Yvette raised a brow. "If you want to ask *where*, *when*, and *who*, just to make sure you've covered the entire W-five, let me in so you're not heating the entire outdoors."

He grumbled but stepped back. Yvette paused inside the door, closing it firmly behind her. She kept her booted feet on the welcome mat while he wandered to the side counter of the neat little kitchen area.

"Looks as if your foot is better."

"Yeah." He took a deep breath and let it out slowly, his shoulders sagging like a deflating balloon. He turned, tilting his head toward the table. "You may as well sit a spell."

Yvette used the bootjack, lining up her boots neatly beside the door before joining him at the table.

He put down a cup of tar-black coffee in a ceramic mug. Thankfully, the offering was followed by a bowl of sugar and rich farm cream—the kind thick enough to stand a spoon in. Yvette sat in the silence and served herself generously from both.

She took a cautious sip. Flavour burst over her tongue, and she gasped.

A very unexpected chuckle drifted across the table. She snapped her gaze up barely in time to catch his brief smile.

"I like simple things." He picked up his own cup and eyed the surface as he gave it a swirl. "Never had much use for fancy doodads, and I raise what I eat. But damn if I didn't go and ruin my taste buds once getting coffee good enough to make the angels sing. Only thing worse than no coffee is bad coffee."

Yvette couldn't stop making noises of approval—although, no way was she telling Tansy that Buns and Roses was no longer *the* coffee spot in town. "You want to teach me how you made this?"

"You don't have family 'round here." The statement rebounded fast and sharp, his gaze tightening as if she'd never asked him a question. As if the peaceful moment was erased.

Yvette would have been in her rights to tell him to mind his own business, but when he stretched out his legs and took another appreciative sip, she paused.

No reason to not answer. It wasn't a secret. "My parents are in Regina. My siblings and their partners and kids as well. My grandparents are here in Heart Falls."

He grunted. "Running wild for a bit before you go home to be with the rest of them?"

She snorted. "Hardly. Just because they live there, that's no reason for me to as well. I like Heart Falls. I like the area and the people. My job." Yvette arched one brow deliberately as she stared right back at him. "Sometimes I even like the people I visit."

He drank deeper, eyeing her over the top of his mug, but didn't say anything.

She didn't try to fill the silence. Instead, she looked around the house and admired the workmanship. Admired the bits of nature scattered everywhere.

The room was quiet, but the silence didn't feel oppressive. It felt as if there was someone else sitting there, speaking into the calmness. Yvette finished her coffee and settled the cup on the table.

All good things had to come to an end, and she figured the peace was one of them. She opened her mouth to ask him about Hunter. About the other animals.

Before she could say a thing, Creighton rose to his feet and gestured to the door. "You need to go," he growled.

Of course, now he chose to get cranky again. "I wanted to talk first."

"Not now." His words rose in volume, and he shook his head. "I'm busy. Don't you fuss."

He left the room.

Marched right into his bedroom and shut the door, leaving her alone in his living room with the fire crackling in the stove and the clock on the wall ticking into the stillness.

Well, that was singularly unhelpful.

She was all the way back in Heart Falls before her phone rang. "Hey, you."

Alex's deep, husky tone streamed into her ear and stroked her libido. "Hey. I know this is last minute, but you want company tonight?"

After her weird afternoon, it would be good to catch him up. "Sure. If you want supper, you have to give me time to pull something out."

"I'll meet you there, and we can cook together. Deal?"

"Perfect."

She pulled in front of the cabin the same moment he did. Alex followed hard on her heels into the living room, rubbing his hands together briskly, blowing on them. "Let me get them warmed up before I kiss you, or you'll be crawling out of your skin."

Yvette didn't try to hide her grin as she closed in on him. "Cold kisses. Would that be another first?"

His eyes flashed. "We've had a few hot ones already," he teased.

His hands rested on her hips as she leaned in. Mouths connecting, the now familiar touch of lips a tease in the split second before Yvette slipped a hand under his T-shirt and planted her icy palm on *his* naked back.

She squealed as he shouted, twisting to try to get away from her. "Christ, woman."

"I'm cold," she complained with a laugh, moving with him to stay in contact. "Boyfriends are supposed to warm up cold hands. I'm sure that's in the rule book."

He tugged her against him and, with one brisk yank, had her shirt separated from her jeans. "Turnabout is fair play."

Icicles pressed to her skin. Only, these had smooth palms and clever fingers, and the next thing Yvette knew, she was missing her shirt and Alex's noticeably warmer hands were all over her.

"Fuck, you feel good." His mouth was back on hers, and she was caught between ripping off his shirt or standing there and enjoying the sensations he was sending through her body. Fingers teasing, circling her nipples over her bra, making her skin come alive.

Dinner—forgotten. Tales of old men and mysterious behaviour—later.

Yvette wanted Alex, and she wanted him now.

She tore her lips back far enough to force out the words. "How starving are you?"

A gasp escaped her hard on the heels of the words, because he'd swung her up in his arms and was carrying her to the bedroom. "Starving."

Flat on her back, body covered by his...

Their booted feet still hanging off the bed.

Yvette grinned at him. "Logistical problems?"

"Fucking clothes. Fuck winter, fuck boots, and just *fuck*." He kissed her again, leaving them both breathless.

Yvette had to admit she'd been sort of expecting a condom to show up in one of the drawers. They were halfway through the month and closing in on the twenty-fifth, and at some point, Alex had to have hoped they would end up here.

Here, sans boots, probably.

Yet there'd been no sign of condoms.

He'd said she got to set the pace, though, So when he kissed her nose and added, "One sec. I'll get us straightened out," Yvette had her own wrangling to do.

The instant he pulled off her boots, she scrambled back on the bed. As he worked to rid himself of his boots, she quickly snatched a condom from the side table where she'd placed it earlier that day, hiding it in her palm.

Innocently, she curled her legs under her then turned to watch as he stripped off his shirt and revealed miles of lean, powerful muscles.

Alex fixed her with a gaze hot enough to melt off her panties. "I could use a taste of what I got the other day."

Yes, please. Plus more. "We could do that. I have another request, as well."

She lifted the condom in the air.

ADRENALINE SHOT through him even as the answer hit his lips. "Yes. Definitely, yes."

She laughed and opened her arms, and they rolled together on the mattress. "You're easy."

"I've been dirty dreaming about being with you for over a year," Alex confessed. He stroked the back of his knuckles along her cheek, loving the flush that rose under his touch. Farther down, he teased, tracing the edge of her bra. Slowly caressing his palm over the tight nub of her nipple. "And when I say dreaming, I mean both the deliberate kind, when my eyes are wide open and I'm using my hand on my cock and imagining it's you surrounding me. Plus, the middle-of-the-night kind, where it's my subconscious going to town with every luscious, body-shaking, spine-tingling kind of fucking possible."

He met her gaze—her eyes wide as she swallowed hard. "That was a touch on the filthy side," she noticed with a breathless whisper.

"You have no idea," he murmured.

He reached behind her and undid her bra, sliding the straps forward and peeling the cups from her breasts. Sweet *fuck*. His mouth watered, and as he slid his palms up her rib cage to capture the heavy mounds, he counted his blessings.

Yvette's eyes fluttered closed as he set his thumbs into a steady rhythm, a circle then gentle scrape with his nails over the peaks.

Her voice was breathy as she demanded, "Use your mouth."

Hallelujah. A woman who asked for what she wanted in bed.

A woman who wanted what he did, even better.

Alex kissed the underside of one breast. Laved his tongue around the outside, slowly closing in on his target.

Yvette took a shaky breath, pressing her hands over his, squeezing tightly. "You're teasing."

"I'm appreciating," he corrected.

She all but growled. "We've been doing really well at not fighting. Don't tell me we're going to mess up our record because you're willing to—*oh, my God*."

His timing was perfect. Lips wrapped around one rosy-red tip, Alex sucked. Hands tightening and relaxing, he appreciated every bit of the heavy swells he held. He flicked his tongue again and again before scraping his teeth over the tight nub, delighted as she gasped.

"Appreciation takes time," he murmured, licking a trail between one breast and the other. "Trust me."

The tension in her body drained away, and she stroked her fingers through his hair. "I want to touch you."

"I want that too." He meant every word of it, but right now he was far too interested in the wonder before him. In the soft colour staining her chest as passion rose. "Goddamn, you're beautiful. I could stay here, teasing and touching." He closed his teeth again, and she jerked against his mouth. "Yeah. Like that. Only, I need even more."

He dragged his teeth off her breasts, leaving a line of moisture all the way down her belly. He stroked his fingers over her sex, moisture coating him instantly as her legs fell apart in welcome.

Her eyes were still closed. At least they were until he slipped his fingertips into her core, brushing his thumb in a gentle rhythm over her sensitive clit.

Her eyelids rose, languid pleasure written there.

"Good?" he asked.

"Oh, yeah." She stretched out one long leg even as she cupped her breasts. Lifting them before taking hold of her nipples between thumb and forefingers.

Alex cursed. "I'm not going to last," he warned.

"Quick on the gun, are you?" she teased.

Minx. The teasing reminder of his last, far-too-rapid trigger made him grin. "Let me remind you about the *I've wanted you for a damn long time* bit."

He needed to up his game, but with how hot she was, the need to keep things rolling was top priority. He increased the pressure on her clit, sliding his fingers in far enough to connect with the front of her passage. Looking for the right spot.

He teased a few times until her inhale turned shaky.

Bingo.

Fingers moving, he eased away far enough to meet her gaze. "Lift your breasts for me."

She offered them up, tight peaks straining toward the ceiling. Alex caught one between his lips, sucking as he speared his fingers deep into her sex.

An easy rhythm landed. One with a dirty soundtrack punctuated with her gasps and moans, her hips pulsing against him, striving for that last little bit.

"*Alex.*"

Her hips rose off the bed, fucking herself against his fingers, and wasn't that the filthiest, most fantastic thing he'd ever seen? Her release exploded from her in a way that made it clear pleasure had started core deep.

He had the condom on faster than proper, soon jerking her leg over his hip and pressing his cock against her sex.

"Look at me," he ordered. "Yes?"

Satisfaction written on her face, a smile curling her lips. "Do it."

Alex flexed his hips, savouring the slow slide of his cock into her body. He paused, taking a deep breath and just feeling.

Yvette's lips quivered, a little moan slipping free. "Oh, that's *good.*"

He drew back slightly then slowly rocked forward. "And this?"

Her chin dipped rapidly. "Wow."

A grin escaped. "*Wow.* I like that. I wonder if I can get a *spectacular* from you?"

She tugged on his shoulders, pulling until his chest rested against her breasts. "You have the most amazing body."

"That's my line." Alex pulsed harder. Sliding her right leg higher over his hip so he could ease in even more. He was slowly but steadily losing his mind, and it felt so damn good.

She kissed his neck, nipping playfully. "Harder."

Hell yes. He braced one arm beside her body and angled upward. Retreating slowly, driving in sharp and deep. Again. Another, chasing noises of pleasure from her lips until his control was thread thin.

She lifted both legs, digging her heels into his buttocks. Leveraging his next thrust to spear herself on his length.

No holds barred. Alex pumped harder as Yvette gasped his name. His spine was melting, and his balls were ready to explode.

When she dragged her nails down his shoulders, he lost it. The pump of her sex squeezing around him dragged loose his release. Spilled pleasure from his body until his arms shook and his hips were all but convulsing.

She tightened around him again, and he swore, their laughter mingling as he let the final pulses strip him dry.

Somehow, he rolled off to land flat on his back beside her. Alex stared at the ceiling, stars swirling in front of his eyes.

Beside him, Yvette panted. He glanced over to enjoy the sight of her breasts quivering with each rapid exhale. Blood was still pooled in far more important parts of his body than his brain, which was probably why it was so damn hard to think.

Yet he was sure something was slightly off.

"What day is it?" he asked.

She laughed, curling up and sliding a hand over his chest. Stroking him as if he were a cat. "The sex was that good, you've lost track of time?"

"Something like that." His amusement grew as the missing piece registered. Sex, today, had been totally Yvette's idea and not spurred on by anything he might have orchestrated.

Which meant the treat he'd planted in her gift calendar was still to come. It should be entertaining when she finally opened that particular drawer to find he'd given her a bunch of condoms as well.

She leaned over and mock glared. "What are you grinning about?"

"Nothing," he insisted innocently. "Want to do it again?"

"Food first." She waggled her brows. "I have leftovers in the freezer we can microwave. We could be back here in under fifteen minutes."

Alex pressed his palms to her cheeks and eased in, kissing her slowly. Thoroughly.

There was no need to rush any of it. The food, the sex. The

conversations. He wanted them to take as much time as necessary. To appreciate every minute as things between them grew better than he'd dreamed possible.

He had to make sure they made it past the finish line and into a future that lasted forever.

12

It seemed opening up the door to a more physical relationship also unlocked a new stage outside the bedroom. Which was equal parts strange and wonderful, yet Yvette was feeling brave enough to simply let things continue to roll.

Alex slipped over to join her at the cabin every time their schedules lined up. Heck, she was pretty sure he was doing some creative fudging when it came to his work hours, but back to that trust thing. He was an adult, and it was his job on the line. If he said he had the time to be with her, she would believe him and enjoy the outright spoiling that followed.

Although it wasn't only about more time together so they could fool around. They talked about things they enjoyed doing. Talked about Creighton and the mystery of his situation. Spent time sharing work stories, and favourite shows and movies. And they'd sang together, which made something inside Yvette warm every single time.

Saturday night, Alex showed up at the cabin along with Brooke and Mack. The guys pulled a propane-powered firepit from the back of his truck and set it up in her yard. Brooke had brought huge wool blankets from the shop, and the four of them sat around the fire and simply enjoyed each other's company.

They also sang, which made Yvette laugh and cry, because while Alex had turned out to have a beautiful voice, and Mack was okay, Brooke was terrible.

They'd tried "Put a Little Holiday in Your Heart," but Brooke stalled out in the middle, laughing too hard to keep going. "I'll just listen to the three of you, okay?"

"That's probably safer." Mack made a face before smiling sheepishly. "I love you."

"I know you do. But you also love your eardrums, so I won't even hurt you for telling me I can't carry a tune in a bucket." She gestured toward Yvette. "You. Be thankful you found a guy who sings nearly as well as you can."

A sweet moment, which turned delightful when Alex and Mack serenaded them both with a little Keith Urban and "I'll Be Your Santa Tonight."

A warm glow surrounded her from more than the fire. Although that contributed to the sweet atmosphere as well.

"This is a cheater fire," Alex teased. "I can only turn it up so high."

"The flames don't need to be three feet high for it to be cozy," Mack drawled. "Besides, I don't know that I've officially approved you for a burn pile. You seem a little irresponsible when it comes to flames and that sort of thing."

Alex stole a hand out from under the covers just long enough to scoop up snow from beside his chair, form it into a snowball, and beam it at Mack.

"Hey," Brooke complained.

"Sorry," Alex offered.

"Not you. Mack." She frowned at her husband. "That snowball broke on your hard head and totally got me wet."

Laughter bloomed, and Mack must've tickled her, because she squirmed, unable to escape.

"Any big plans for the holidays?" Brooke asked when she could speak again.

"Dropping in on my grandma and grandpa." Yvette stalled out.

Well, *shoot*. She hadn't asked Alex if they had plans for an official Christmas Day celebration. Only, she wasn't about to bring that up right now.

He found her fingers under the blankets, squeezing them tight. "I'll be working at Silver Stone for the morning. Ashton volunteered to be on duty at the fire hall."

"That's nice of him," Yvette said. She frowned. "I thought he spent the day with the Stone family."

"You'd think he'd want to spend the day with Sonora," Mack grumbled softly before coughing into his fist as if he hadn't said anything.

The four of them grinned at each other before Alex spoke again, a little slower, as if considering his words. "Maybe he asked and she said no. She'll have her grandchildren and kids to spend time with. Who knows what's happening with them?"

"As long as we're not going to pretend that there's *nothing* happening," Mack said.

Yvette was still figuring out where to go regarding Christmas Day and Alex. How had it so completely slipped her mind that she—no, that *they* hadn't talked about this already?

A message alert buzzed, and she pulled out her phone to peer at the screen. Making sure it wasn't a vet emergency.

Ugh. Her sister. Definitely not a call to bother with right now, especially since the message started with, *I can't believe you did that.*

She tucked the phone away.

By the time Brooke and Mack packed up to leave and Alex

was following Yvette into the house, her sister had messaged a half dozen times.

When Yvette deliberately placed her phone facedown on the table, Alex raised a brow. "Do you want me to keep ignoring the fact that you're ignoring someone else? Or do you want to talk?"

"I'd prefer to take you to my room and have my wicked way with you," Yvette confessed.

Alex caught her by the fingers and led her to the couch, sitting and pulling her into his lap. "I like the sex, but I also like the rest of what we're doing. Time with our friends, time together."

She sighed. "Time when I confess that my sister is a shit and I spend a lot of energy avoiding her?"

The confusion on his face was wiped away quickly. "Oh. The phone? I'm sorry."

"Me too." She laid her head on his shoulder, stroking her fingers over the rough stubble on his chin. "She's not truly evil or anything. But she's not very nice, either."

"I've had people in my life like that." He pressed his lips to her temple, and a warm bubble of affection wrapped itself around her.

"Some of the foster kids you spent time with?"

"Yes." He hummed for a moment then nodded, as if making a decision. "I told you Hans and Glenda were amazing parents. I can honestly say I never once felt as if they picked and chose favourites. They just wanted to be there for as many kids as possible. Some of those kids needed a little more attention, but I wasn't neglected, even if I wasn't the center of attention."

The words went straight to the heart of the matter, poking both her guilty conscience and her frustrated nerves.

"You're doing that mind-reading thing again," Yvette warned. She wiggled to change position until she had her own section of the couch, pillows stuffed behind her back, feet resting in his lap. "My parents definitely picked favourites. I think that's part of what Grandma and Grandpa didn't approve of."

"Ah. Your sister?"

"Her, rotating through my brothers at different times. Everything was about appearances in our family." Thinking back to some of those childhood years was unpleasant. She met Alex's eyes. "In some ways, I admire my siblings. They're all fantastic businesspeople, they're personable in public, and they get stuff done."

"You just described you as well," he said softly.

"I know that. But my *get stuff done* didn't involve a career on the approved list. Becoming a veterinarian didn't add to the financial bottom line of the family—*they're* all involved in some sort of house building or selling or improvement venue. *Build your home the Wright way.* My part-time job as a dog walker when I was a teen didn't get the Wright name in the newspaper or mentioned on the radio. Not like when my three brothers, while still teenagers, built a Habitat for Humanity house by themselves, or when my sister won Miss Shag Carpet."

Alex blinked. "Tell me that's not a thing."

She snickered softly. "Sorry, that was me being rude. But she did win some other pageant that was held during a home-improvement fair. And you don't have to reassure me that I'm beautiful, because I like how I look. I just wasn't *enough*. And it might sound terrible, but after being told I was too forward or too quiet, or that I was lazy, immediately followed by too obsessed—I needed to get out of there."

A soft curse drifted from his lips. He was rubbing her legs now, anger at the back of his eyes. "They were gaslighting you."

"I know that now. Carrie does it the most. Which is why I'm ignoring her, because somehow, whatever it is she wants to talk to me about? It'll be my fault that something's wrong, or how

VIVIAN AREND

dare I not get it to her yesterday, and why am I so difficult when she's always wanted nothing but the best for me?"

"Oh, sweetheart. That sucks."

Alex was watching her closely, absolutely no judgment on his face. Which was why the next words spilled free.

"I feel guilty."

Instantly he shook his head. "Oh, hell no. Nobody deserves to do things that make you feel bad. Especially not family."

"But *I'm* doing everything I can to avoid my family. And then I see you, who gave up your job and moved back home to do everything for your parents. I can't even pick up the phone to call my parents. I'm a terrible daughter."

"Bullshit." Not only was his volume up, but his eyes flashed with the closest thing to fury she'd seen in a long time. "That's complete and utter bullshit, and you do not get to put that kind of crap on yourself."

"It's how I feel," Yvette protested.

"Because too many times, this damn world teaches us that's what we're supposed to feel. But you know those parents I gave up so much to go help? One of the first things they taught me was that feelings are only something we should listen to when they're *right*. Because when I showed up on their doorstep, eight years old and feeling as if I must be the worst kid on the face of the earth because even my mother didn't want me, they told me feelings can lie."

Something tightened inside Yvette's heart and at the back of her throat. "I'm so sorry."

For the little boy he'd been. For the hurt that must have caused.

For the ridiculousness of worrying about her small-time complaints when he'd had his world torn apart while so young and innocent.

"You're sorry?" His gaze tightened. "Forget that noise. I mean, yes, it was terrible I had to go through that, but I ended up with Hans and Glenda, and my world changed. That's not something to be sorry for, that's a thing to celebrate."

"I'm glad." Although she was definitely going to pin her lips together and stop feeling sorry for herself.

"Good. So now you can just knock any fucked-up ideas from your head that are saying *I don't get to complain because Alex had it so much worse than me...*"

He was downright creepy at times. "How did you—?"

"How do I know? It's in your eyes, sweetheart." He touched his finger to her temple. "You look as if you want to crawl away and hide, but that's not happening. Not unless there's enough room in your blanket fort for both of us."

Yvette stopped and tried a mental reset.

He was correct—again.

The things in her life that weren't right *were* important. He cared enough to want her to be honest. "I know feelings can lie. I mean, I know it in my head, but it's not sunk in completely, because the feelings are still there."

He sat up, her hands held tight in his. "Then it's time to do something about that. Talk to me, talk to a therapist. Talk to your friends, but *talk*. Hell, you should shout, cry, *scream*, until things change."

She couldn't say anything, so she simply nodded because he was right. She agreed completely.

She just wasn't sure how to get from where she was to where she needed to go.

They sat quietly. Then Alex spoke softly. "Here's one thing I don't get. I've worked with you when you're on the job. You're downright cheeky. You're bold, and you're proud and solid, even when you're dealing with the biggest assholes out there. And farmers, let's be blunt, are assholes."

That stole a chuckle from her, wobbly as it was.

He gathered her up so she was once again sitting in his lap. He pushed a loose strand of hair behind her ear. "I contrast that confidence with how you are sometimes when I ask you an innocent question. Or now, when you talk about dealing with your terrible family. Why does it throw you for such a loop? Any ideas?"

She paused, but the first thing that shot to mind was a truth she'd suspected for a long time. "I did it on my own. When I went to veterinarian school, I did it *in spite* of what they wanted. The whole time I was there, it was just me. No older siblings with their shining reputations to live up to. No bad behaviors from their past I had to prove to be better than. For the first time, I got to be *Yvette* instead of someone's younger sister or Kent and Kim's daughter. I'm solid as a professional. It's just... relationships, not so much."

He nodded. "That makes sense."

She hated that their wonderful evening had turned into this. Her, with tears threatening to fall. But then again...

She caught Alex's fingers and pressed them to her lips. "This sucks."

A laugh escaped. "Yes, it does."

No, he didn't get what she meant. She needed to be brave enough to ensure he did.

She tried again because this was too important to let slide. "This sucks, but I'm glad you're here. I'm glad I'm on the verge of crying my eyes out and you're here. Being together changes things. It *means* things. It means *everything*." Tears were coming now, but she held them back for long enough to finish, eyes locked on his as she shared the final truth. "It means everything that we're together."

ALEX HAD SEEN MORE baby animals brought into this world than he could count. There was always a moment of wonder when the foal or the calf, or even a chick escaping their shell, would totter up on wobbly legs. He recognized that moment. Observing their shaky new steps into a brand-new world.

Which meant he was awestruck to be there in that moment, witnessing as Yvette took some brand-new shaky steps into her future.

He curled his arms around her and squeezed tight. He didn't say anything yet. Figured what she needed first was to let those tears out. The ones that were dropping hard and fast as if she'd been holding them in for years.

Damn if his eyes weren't a little weepy as well.

Together—hell, just thinking the word made something inside him light up with all kinds of hope.

He stroked her shoulders for a bit until the sobs turned to sniffles then to steadily smoother breaths.

"I need to get up for a minute." Yvette wiggled forward and off his lap.

He let her go so she could blow her nose and wipe her eyes, but it was immensely satisfying when she returned and immediately crawled back into his arms.

Rocking back, he put his feet up on the coffee table. The soft, warm woman in his arms fit perfectly against him. The logs crackled in the fireplace, light shining on the pretty trinkets she had on display all around her house. The cabin was cozy—but not quite somewhere Alex could see living with her.

But moving in together was a problem for another time, because he needed to finish their conversation.

"What happens now?" Alex asked. "Because I want to support you, especially if you need to make tough choices. Only, I don't want to barrel you down some path you don't want to go."

She rubbed her hand against his chest, a wry smile on her lips. "There's a part of me that keeps being optimistic. Thinking that if I answer Carrie, it'll magically end up a normal conversation. That she'll be sweet and loving like Lisa and her sisters. But I've been proved wrong too many times before."

"You want to tell me about it so you can get it off your chest, or do you want to do some problem-solving? Because I can do either. A sympathetic ear or a brainstorm session."

"Brainstorming is a good idea." She wrinkled her nose. "We should be armed with a full table of Tansy's baked goods before we dive in, though."

He laughed softly. "We can put it off until we're loaded with carbs, but will you be able to just ignore her?"

As if punctuating his sentence, another text message arrived, her phone vibrating on the table.

Yvette all but growled. "Here's where I get trapped in this endless loop. I start thinking about what I should do, and it backfires. Because what if I block Carrie's number, but she's actually trying to get a hold of me because something's happened to my parents or brothers?"

"How many times in the past fifteen years has that happened?" Alex asked.

Yvette opened her mouth then closed it, a crease forming between her brows. "*Ummm.*"

He leaned in and brushed his lips over hers. "My quick advice. Block her phone number, because from what you've said, she lost the privilege of contacting you a long time ago. Set up an email you give only to your family, and they can use that. Get somebody you trust, like Brooke, to preview the emails. She can delete them if there's anything toxic, and you can respond only to the things that are absolutely necessary. Or ignore them if it's just nonsense that you don't need to acknowledge. Being family doesn't give them the right to any of your time or energy."

Her expression grew thoughtful. "If I have time and energy to spend making a difference in people's lives, I want it to be here in Heart Falls. You know, like maybe encouraging Ashton and Sonora to get their act together. Or helping take care of someone cranky but harmless like Creighton, who doesn't have anyone else in his life." She cringed. "I still feel horrid saying that. Because it's like saying my family isn't worth the effort."

"It needs to sink in that this didn't start with choices you made," Alex said softly. "Honestly? It's okay to feel terrible."

"Really?"

"Just a little." He nodded. "Only for a short while. Because feeling that way would be a reminder that you're doing the right thing for yourself for a change. If it feels bad to take care of your own heart, then, okay. I'd prefer that rather than you feeling terrible because they worked you over and left you bruised."

"That makes sense." She still didn't look very happy.

Alex tucked his fingers underneath her chin. "Just so you know, I'm not brilliant, pulling that idea out of thin air. It was a solution I had to use with one of my former foster brothers. A tactic I did on recommendation from my parents."

Her lips curled into a circle. "Oh."

"Yes, oh." He kissed her because he simply couldn't not.

She straightened suddenly. "Brooke reminded me of something. I can't believe I forgot to ask, but what are your plans for Christmas? You said you have to work in the morning. Do you want to spend the day together?"

Oh, boy. Did he ever. "Yup. You going to go see your grandparents? Can I join you?"

She nodded, a pleased smile washing away the final bits of sadness. "After lunch is the traditional gift-opening time. Then, if you want, you can come back here, and we can cook something festive."

He was on the verge of asking if she wanted to FaceTime with his parents but decided to hold off for now. With everything else going on, it was okay to let that part—the meet-the-parents part—ease in a little slower. "Sounds like a perfect holiday plan."

Then she slid her fingers into his hair, and he became the kissee. Text messages forgotten, the tension and sadness of the past hour slipped away as she pulled him into her bedroom then moved them together.

That word again. *Together*.

It meant so much more than ever before. It wasn't only about tangled limbs and sweaty body parts, the sheets on her bed shoved aside as they teased and stroked and offered each other pleasure.

It was the bits of laughter that rose between them. Like when he rolled her on top then damn near squawked in surprise, curling upright to discover a key chain had slid under his back. "What's this doing here?"

Her cheeks flushed as she confessed, "It's for tomorrow. I sleep with the next day's key under my pillow."

It was the little sounds she made as he curled himself around her, slipping on a condom and sliding deep. It was him reaching down to press his thumb over her clit as the storm between them rushed higher until they both broke.

Together.

Beyond that night, *together* meant striving to find time where they could talk, laugh, and just be. Alex did everything he could to be there every day when she opened the daily calendar drawer.

Monday, four days before Christmas, he stood beside her on the porch, both of them wrapped from head to toe against the bitter cold. "They really should hold Christmas sometime in the summer," Yvette complained.

"They do. In New Zealand," Alex drawled as she opened the drawer and peeked in. Peals of laughter exploded from her, and he leaned closer to see what had happened. "What?"

She slid her fingers into the narrow space and pinched,

lifting out a ribbon-wrapped five-pack of condoms. "You *did* give me condoms. Now I know why you were so confused when I offered one up days ahead of schedule."

He wasn't sure why she was laughing so hard, but it seemed appropriate to tease. "Oh, these aren't for sex. I thought we could make balloon animals out of them or something, for entertainment."

She grinned then peeked in the drawer again, pulling out the next day's key, plus the note he'd included and the bar of decadent dark chocolate. She popped open the envelope.

These are for when you're ready. In the meantime, I want you to feel good, and they do say chocolate is the nearest thing to an orgasm.

Amusement danced over her face. "Not for sex?"

"I figured you'd really get off on balloon animals."

Which started another set of laughter, this one not leading to the bedroom but inside the house, next to the fire, where they sat on the loveseat he'd pulled into position so they could stay warm and cuddled together, both reading quietly for the next while. Connected. Something growing deeper and richer.

As if something magical was approaching every day closer they got to Christmas.

13

*A*lex wondered if he should wrap Yvette's final gift, or leave it out, in case he needed to add anything before Friday. The present was one he'd had no opportunity to work on prior to arriving in Heart Falls, but it was going to be a hit with her. He already knew it.

Plus, there was the final drawer in the Christmas calendar, and a surprise she didn't know about. He wanted Christmas Day to be a perfect opportunity to take what they were doing and slide their relationship to the next stage.

Two days to go. He didn't want to be overly cocky, but so far, so good.

His phone rang. "Hey, Dad. Hey, Mom."

"Just me this time," Hans said with a hearty laugh. "Your mom is out on a trail ride with the new foster kids Caitlin and Aaron got this past weekend. Three of them. Ten, eight, and seven. All of them wound up tighter than old-fashioned tops. I think your sister plans to bounce all the sadness out of them."

"They arrived? I thought they wouldn't be there for another week. That's what Aaron said when he messaged me yesterday."

They both knew with fostering, the kids arrived when they needed to arrive. Or a little later than they should have.

His dad's tone of voice said he understood what was going through Alex's head. "Change of plans. So we'll have a bigger group for the holidays. Can't say I'm disappointed."

"No, I guess not." Alex could picture it now. His mom and dad in their glory, handing out presents and hugs and as much attention as the new kids needed. "Good to hear you didn't try to join in riding yet."

"Pain in the ass that I can't, but I'm enjoying the new hip and no pain far too much to complain about having to take it easy."

"You've never been the type to complain." Alex let the memories of everything this man had done for him wash over him in a happy wave. The truth hit so hard, it nearly bowled him over. "What you've got is special. You and Mom. I'm very thankful to be your son."

A faint pause, and then his dad hummed happily. "Don't know what brought that on but can't say I'm disappointed. We love you. Glad to know the tough days were worth it."

"Every one of them," Alex acknowledged.

Every time the goodness of his past struck him, he realized all over again what a fool he'd been when it came to Yvette and his teasing ways over the past years. She didn't have the same rock-solid base he'd built on. Being grateful for what he had growing up wasn't enough. He needed to somehow be able to pass that blessing on to her, and others.

"Did I lose you, or are you sitting there thinking deep thoughts?" his dad asked softly.

"I'm still here," Alex said. "But definitely falling into that deep-thought place."

"You want solutions, or you just want to talk it out?"

Alex chuckled. "I said that to someone the other day and instantly thought of you."

"Good to know something sank in," his dad teased. "This to do with that sweetie of yours?"

"Yep. Things are going well, or at least I think they are. She's pretty special, Dad. I'm sure we're right for each other. But one moment it looks as if it should just be smooth sailing, and then..." Alex took a deep breath. "I'm not asking you for dating advice, though. Definitely not."

A loud burst of laughter escaped his father. "Then I'm definitely not giving you any."

"Because you and Mom have been together forever, but that doesn't mean that you can shove my feet the right direction."

Alex could picture his father shaking his head silently, wondering if he should pull out a two-by-four to help get things through his son's solid head.

"This is me not giving you any advice. You thinking it's right is not enough. Do you know this woman? Does she know *you*? Are you growing and learning together? That's the part that makes it last. That's what you need to work on."

"I'm trying." Alex wasn't about to list all the things he was doing. But still, his father's voice carried on, and the words stole deep.

"Are you listening to what's important to her?" Hans asked.

Yvette had shared so much over the past week. All of it important. All things Alex had tried to support her—

Creighton.

"Oh."

On the other end of the line, his dad cleared his throat, amusement clear. "What was that? You swallow a fly over there?"

Alex nearly held up a hand to keep his father from talking before he lost the thought. "I'll call you back."

He hung up, certain his dad was laughing hard and shaking his head right now. But that wasn't the thing to focus on.

Creighton. Yvette had said something in passing while they were talking about her family. How she'd prefer to be spending her energy helping local people. She'd been doing her best to deal with the old man—which had nothing to do with being professional.

For some reason, she cared about him. Cared about making a difference.

Didn't matter that Alex didn't get why this particular individual had become such a thing, but he was. What's more, wanting to help the old man was her pushing forward in a *relationship* setting. An area that made her uncomfortable, but she had stuck with it.

Seems she was attempting some self-therapy all along.

Which meant a good boyfriend should encourage her with that task. Maybe even lend a helping hand.

Not that he wanted to take over, but there were all the questions currently buzzing around town. He and Yvette suspected the old man was quietly dropping his animals off with others.

Why?

Ignoring everything else, Alex bundled his way out of his bunkhouse room and headed up the mountain.

The temperature was well below freezing. While it was supposed to warm up by the afternoon, the frigid cold from the night lingered, and it wasn't until Alex spotted the thin thread of smoke rising from Creighton's chimney that a little of the worry inside eased. Whatever else was up, the old man was at least keeping up with day-to-day activities.

Alex had barely put his knuckles to the door when Creighton hauled the door open.

"Get in here before I lose all the heat," the old man grumbled.

One of the dogs who'd usually acted as part of the greeting committee looked up from the pillow in the corner of the room, tail beating out a rhythm as he stared hopefully at Alex.

But he stayed put until Creighton called him over.

Alex used the excuse of petting the dog to look away from the old man. "It's cold. I figured I'd come and make sure everything was all right."

The man returned to the table and pulled a straight-backed chair out, the back legs dragging over the wooden floor. "Bullshit."

Alex motioned the dog back to the corner and joined Creighton at the table. "What makes you say that?"

Creighton pushed the coffee urn toward him plus an empty cup. "Because I've lived here for a hell of a long time, and you've never come to check up on me before. Which makes me think it's that woman of yours who put you up to it."

Alex shrugged. "You're a smart man but only partly right. First, it's more like she's the one in charge, and I belong to her. Second, she didn't put me up to anything, but I know she's thinking about you. So I figured I'd do her a solid and save her a trip up your god-awful road."

Creighton grinned. "Didn't take you for a wimp."

"Did you lose a bet when you were building it?" Alex drawled with amusement. "Because, hell, that road just makes no sense to nobody."

The old man took a shaky breath, unexpected in the midst of the good-natured teasing. He stared at the table. "It's all going sideways."

Alex waited.

Creighton pressed both palms to the table. "I thought I could soldier on. I like living out here. I like my place and everything I built with my two hands. Even my god-awful road, but it's all falling apart."

"Falling apart, or getting to be too much?" Alex asked simply.

Then, dear God, if Creighton didn't start crying. A thin sound escaping him like air from a balloon.

The dog in the corner was there in an instant, head resting in Creighton's lap, tail wagging.

Alex sat quietly, drinking his coffee until the old man got himself back together.

Wrinkled hands traced a smooth pattern over the dog's head, again and again. Even the trembling in the man's fingers said something—he cared. He cared a hell of a lot.

Creighton wiped the back of his hand against his eyes. "Didn't see that Hunter was feeling down. And then the vet says I should take better care of him. Felt like a slap, but when he died a few days later, I realized she was right."

Alex laid a hand on the man's shoulder. "Yvette told me Hunter was old, and there wasn't much you could do. He had a good life. Bet he enjoyed chasing a hell of a lot of rabbits over the years. Don't you put yourself down about it being his time to go."

"Fine, but it was a wake-up call. If I can't take care of them, I've got no right to have the beasts."

"You've been dropping them off at various places in town, haven't you?"

The old man nodded. He glanced up at Alex. "She's a good one, that lady of yours. I'm not the easiest to get along with, yet every time she came up here, she's been respectful and smart. Wish I had a daughter like her."

Alex honest-to-God grinned. "Hearing that would make her proud. I know she likes you too, cranky bastard that you are."

Creighton snorted. "I don't know if I like you at all, though." But he smiled.

It was time for the next thing.

"What do you need?" Alex asked.

The old man leaned back slightly in his chair, still patting the head of the old dog, the beast staring at him with absolute adoration. "It's time I got my own carcass somewhere a little simpler to handle. I've had my name on the wait list at the seniors' home down in Heart Falls. Seems they've got room for me and Tex—a private apartment. I still get to take care of myself best I can, but if I tip over the line, there'll be people to help me up."

Alex stared at him in amazement. "You're moving to the Heart Falls senior lodge? Just like that?"

"Yup."

Holy hell. Not that he wanted to jinx this or anything, but still. "You're acting awfully reasonable," he pointed out cautiously. "I figure I'll be peeling my father's fingers off the farmhouse doorframe to get him to leave when it's time."

A gentle lift of the old man's shoulders indicated his acceptance of the idea. "You just said it. *When it's time.* It's time. I've seen the writing on the wall."

Well. There wasn't much more to be said then.

Alex slapped his hands together. "Okay. You let me know what I can do to help you."

Creighton pushed back his chair and pointed toward the door. Two suitcases and a couple of boxes were stacked to the right. "There's my stuff. I'd be obliged if you'd give me a ride."

"Right now? *Today?*"

A chuckle rose from the man. "You're not quite as quick on the uptake as your girl, are you?"

"I'm just surprised," Alex admitted. "How did you know I was going to show up?"

Creighton pulled on his coat, slipped on boots, and put his cowboy hat in place. "Didn't. I was going to give Yvette a call in a bit. So you saved her a trip up that god-awful road, just like you hoped."

Wonders would never cease. Now the man was *teasing* him.

"You need anything else from here?"

Creighton shook his head. "Later. I left an envelope there with instructions. Let's get this over with. They said I could join the chow line tonight. It'll be the first time somebody else has cooked for me in more years than I can remember."

Alex stacked the boxes in the back of the crew cab, returning for the final suitcase.

Creighton pivoted slowly on his front porch, nodding as he took a final look around. Then he pulled the door shut behind him and made his way to the passenger seat of the truck. Tex curled up at his feet, head resting on Creighton's knee.

The trip to town was quiet. Not that Alex didn't have a million questions he wanted to ask, but he figured Creighton deserved to be able to have a say in his own time.

They were just about at the seniors' lodge when Creighton cleared his throat. "You don't mess things up with that young lady. You hear me? You treat her good."

"I plan to," Alex assured him. "As far and fast as she'll let me."

A satisfied grunt escaped the other man. Then they were carrying boxes into his modestly furnished apartment.

Alex's phone was burning a hole in his back pocket, and he wanted to check in with Yvette and let her know the astonishing changes of the day. But he focused on Creighton, because that's what she would've wanted. Helping bring in his things and getting the old man settled. Or at least started on the way.

Creighton gave him an assessing stare. "Seems there's one more thing I need you to do."

"Anything," Alex offered.

Creighton then pointed to one of the hardback chairs at his new table. An actual ear-to-ear grin brightened his lined face. "You're going to need to sit down for this one."

Yvette could not find hide nor hair of Alex. He wasn't answering her calls, and her last text messages had gone unanswered.

She grumbled as she slid into the Heart Falls Auto Shop in search of Brooke. "Not much good having the afternoon off when I can't *find* the man."

Her friend popped up from behind the desk, wiping grease from her fingers on a not-too-clean rag. "You lost someone? Oh, I know. Old Saint Nick—you're trying to track him down so you can ask for the perfect Christmas present."

"More like trying to figure out what to *give* for the perfect Christmas present." Yvette shook her head in annoyance. "I can't believe it, but it's two days before Christmas, and I still don't have anything for Alex."

Brooke blinked in surprise. "Really?"

Guilt rolled in again, but this time Yvette figured she was allowed to embrace the emotion. "I'm a terrible girlfriend."

Her friend's smile flashed back into place. "From the way he was raving about you to Mack the other day at the fire hall, Alex is pretty happy with you as a girlfriend."

Which sent a lovely quiver off in her belly. "You did hear the part where I don't have a present for him and Christmas is in two days. Yes?"

Brooke gestured her around the side of the counter. "Did you guys talk about presents at all?"

Yvette settled in a waiting room chair hard enough, it groaned. "Oh, well, no. Even though every single day, I've been opening a gift that *he* gave me."

A light smack on the back of her arm brought Yvette's attention up to see Brooke giving her the evil eye. "That whole gift calendar thing is cool, but it's not the same as you realizing you want to give the man something special, which is what I think I'm hearing you say."

"I should've clued in earlier—"

Yvette interrupted herself. An echo of a voice inside insisted she'd been inconsiderate. Thinking only of herself.

A voice that sounded suspiciously like her mother or her sister.

But it wasn't true. Yvette *had* been thinking, only every time she'd come up with an idea, it hadn't been right. It hadn't been the thing that was going to make Alex the happiest.

Time to buckle down. Yvette dipped her chin firmly "We need to focus on a solution and not me beating myself up."

Brooke squeezed Yvette's fingers. "That's my girl. Tell me what you've put on the reject pile, and we'll come up with something good."

The sparkle in her friend's eyes as they worked through a list was another layer of proof that Yvette had made good choices. Coming to Heart Falls, finding people she cared about and who cared about her—it was right. It was good, and she was going to enjoy every minute of it fully.

Including scrambling last minute to put together a present that Alex would truly appreciate.

She knew the minute they nailed down the idea. "You realize I now have to go talk to Ashton."

Brooke waved her off. "Go. I love you too much to make you sit here when you look excited enough to fly with the reindeer."

Stopping at Silver Stone and tracking down Ashton only took another fifteen minutes. He was currying his favourite horse, the long peaceful sweeps of his arm mesmerizing to watch.

Yvette cleared her throat. "Mind if I interrupt?"

He paused then dipped his chin. "You need my full attention, or can I finish working on Happy-Go-Lucky here?"

"Keep working. I need some information on Alex," she said quickly. "Personal stuff, which I know you can't usually hand out, but I'm really hoping you'll be okay bending the rules a little."

Ashton hesitated for a second before his fingers went back into motion. "Personal?"

Yvette glanced around to make sure no one else was in hearing distance then explained, finishing up quickly with, "What do you think?"

He breathed in deep, letting it out slowly. "Let me finish. I've got that information on file." Ashton flashed a rare grin, amusement rising. "I take it he's convinced you to keep going past December?"

"It was kind of hard to not be convinced. Not when the man pretty much started out telling me he thought we were supposed to be together."

Ashton's expression went serious. "Was that all it took?"

Yvette wasn't ready to explain further. Not before she'd told Alex the truths she'd discovered.

But the man looked honestly interested, and for one moment, she thought of Sonora and Alex's cryptic comment that maybe it wasn't Ashton holding back.

She considered hard then shared the one thing she could. "What I thought I needed a month ago is not what I truly needed. Alex has given me the time to figure that out, all the while making it very clear what *he* needs. We've still got stuff to work out in the future, but I think we plan to do it together."

The older man's gruff expression didn't change much, but he did brush his hands off and motioned toward the door. "Let me get that info for you."

Only minutes later, she crawled into her truck and made a nerve-wracking call. She'd just finished when her phone vibrated.

A text message from work, which sent her driving back across town to her house and the veterinarian office that was closed for the holidays, except for emergencies.

"Josiah? You in?" Yvette stepped toward the back of the clinic.

He wandered out from the examination room, smile brightening as he spotted her. "Yvette. Great, thanks for stopping in. I need you to do a run for me to Creighton's. Something about one of the dogs he's worried about."

"Okay."

He paused. "You're not going to complain?"

She shrugged lightly. "We've been getting along. I actually have something for him."

She'd gotten Creighton a Christmas present even while she'd been struggling to find one for Alex.

Josiah let out a relieved sigh. "Thank you so much for doing this. With the temperature finally rising and snow on the way, Lisa's family is having us out to Red Boot ranch for tobogganing. I didn't want to miss it."

"Of course not. Glad I could help," Yvette insisted.

He headed toward the door. "I have something for you. I'll tuck it in the back of your truck. You can grab it later."

The snow Josiah had mentioned arrived with a vengeance between her pausing to grab Creighton's gift and heading out.

Huge, puffy flakes swirled downward like someone was shaking feather pillows over the landscape, turning it into a winter wonderland. It didn't matter that, underneath, there were miles of yellow-brown stubble in the fields. Couldn't tell that a week ago, the roads had been a muddy mess, rutted and slimy.

This was the time of year where brand-new beginnings arrived with each fresh snowfall. A glittering white surface to start afresh.

She didn't get suspicious until she drove into the yard and discovered Alex's truck parked just past Creighton's beater.

The two younger dogs came running to greet her, bouncing in circles until she tossed them treats. Then they beelined it back to the barn. Neither of them looked as if they needed veterinary attention.

She climbed the steps up to the porch and knocked. "Creighton? It's Yvette. I'm coming in."

The door swung open, a rush of heat and the scent of gingersnaps sliding over her. But it wasn't her cranky old farmer waiting for her in the cozy little cabin.

It was Alex.

14

The expression on Yvette's face made Alex grin all the harder. "As Creighton would say, come and sit a spell."

Her lips twitched. "I have so many questions, but let's start with, *where is he*?"

Alex shook his head. "That's not a very good place to start. How about I ask you a question first? Did Josiah give you something to bring with you?"

She frowned. "Yes?"

"Fantastic. Stay here, and I'll be right back."

He moved fast, but he still had a layer of snow on his head and shoulders by the time he returned from grabbing the package.

Yvette had taken off her coat and boots, but she remained standing awkwardly in the kitchen area. Alex marched past her and put the package on the counter then turned and gathered her in his arms.

"Hi."

She ruffled his hair, and a snowstorm flew around them. "Hi."

"Answers second, kisses first," he murmured before leaning in and taking another taste of what he so desperately needed. The sweetness of her fingers locked around the back of his neck, the tease of her tongue against his. The curl of her smile against his lips before they broke apart.

He took a moment to remove his coat and boots, passing her a pair of slippers. "We may as well get comfy."

Her gaze darted all around the room, but she sat in a kitchen chair and obediently pulled on the set of moccasin-like slippers. "Are you going to get around to the point where you explain what's going on?"

He'd had a good solid hour to plan how to sum it up, and it still hadn't been enough. "Stay sitting."

She arched a brow. "That bad?"

"Honestly, that good." He handed her the letter that had been propped up on the kitchen table. "At the risk of making a long story too short, Creighton has decided to move—no, let me try that again. Creighton *has* moved into town, as of today. As of like two hours ago. I drove him into town, and he is now living there. He wants to sell his place to you."

"What?" She blinked in confusion, fingers fumbling to open the letter as if hoping it would make more sense than what he'd just announced. "He *moved*? Then how come I'm supposed to take a look at one of his dogs, neither of which seem to need to be looked at?"

"That's my fault," Alex confessed. "I needed a way to get you up here, and Josiah offered to send you on a job."

She slid the paper from the envelope and unfolded it. She smoothed it on the table as Alex stepped behind her, leaning down to wrap his arms around her waist as they both read the words he'd already examined earlier.

Ms. Wright
Dr. Wright

Yvette

I remember the first time you came out here. I thought Josiah had a baby sister he'd brought along for the ride. You had these braids poking out from underneath your cowboy hat, and you looked about twelve years old.

Only, when you and him got to talking about the animals, I couldn't understand half the words that came out of your mouth. That's when I realized you were a whole hell of a lot smarter than me.

You didn't act like you were better than me. No matter how terrible I was, you stuck to your guns and treated me, and my animals, with respect.

I'll admit I'm not the easiest man to get along with. Stubborn, willful. Pretty damn set in my ways, and quite content with how I've lived my life. The only thing I never did accomplish was finding someone to spend my life with. Never got to raise a family.

There are plenty of times, when a man's by himself, he gets to thinking and wonders what might've been. I think about all the times you came up here on your own and I was extra cranky, so you rightly sassed me off and told me exactly what I needed to do, yet never raised your voice—

I ain't planning on writing a novel. You're a fine veterinarian. You're a good person. If I did have any kids, I would've wanted them to be like you.

So now that I can't live out here anymore, I'll let you have first dibs at purchasing my land. You still need to pay me, because I'm no fool. But I only need enough to live comfortably, and I don't mind getting it in a few chunks, if that's easier for you. I left the price I'm willing to accept on the next page.

I hope you'll take care of the dogs, no matter what. Tex is old, and quiet, and his bones will enjoy retiring with me to the new place in town. The other two are too full of vim and vigour still to be happy anywhere except outdoors.

Thanks for all you've done for me over the years. Because I know I didn't say it enough.

You give it some thought about buying the farm, then come see me.

Your friend,
Creighton Reiner

Yvette twisted in her chair as Alex settled next to her, holding her hand.

She was still staring at the letter, shuffling underneath for the second page. A gasp escaped her. "He wants me to buy his place. But that's not nearly what it's worth. He may as well be giving it away."

"Which is what he would do if he could," Alex said softly. "It's quite a compliment. That he thinks so much if you, he basically wants you to inherit his life's work."

Shock danced in her eyes, but her lips curled upward slightly. She took a deep breath and nodded. "Yes, that is a compliment. I still can't believe it's true."

"Give it some time to sink in. Let me tell you about the other reason you're here," he offered.

Her smile twisted again. "Please do."

He held her hand, brushing his thumb back and forth over the pulse point of her wrist. "You have the rest of the day and all of tomorrow off. By some strange coincidence, so do I."

He leaned in and pressed his lips to her cheek. To her jaw. To the sweet spot under her ear.

"Go on," she purred. "This sounds intriguing."

"Well. Since we've both got nowhere we have to be, I thought maybe we could take a good look around what could possibly become your new home. See what you think, make lists of pros and cons. Also, get a really good massage from your boyfriend."

"All of that sounds pretty wonderful," Yvette said before tilting her head and asking him playfully, "Where is *go hungry because there's nothing to eat* on this schedule?"

"Oh, ye of little faith." Alex motioned toward the kitchen. "I brought supplies. I brought music. We both have books to read —I picked up your new gruesome tome from Fallen Books."

She snickered.

He winked. "Plus enough food, including bacon, for us to stay until I have to go on shift Saturday morning. That bag is your clothes. Brooke slipped over to your place and packed it for you then dropped it off with Josiah."

"Sneaky."

"Yup. And in case you're wondering, I also brought fresh bedsheets and a large pack of condoms."

Laughter filled the small cabin. The happy sound bounced off the walls and echoed back into his heart.

She slid a hand against his cheek, examining his face as if trying to memorize every line. "I would love to stay here with you."

Sheer happiness flooded through him, and before he realized what he was doing, he was on his feet, tugging her to the soft rug he'd tossed in front of the wood-burning stove.

He gathered her in his arms, just sitting together as the heat slid over them, his thoughts in a whirl.

Yvette kept turning her head slowly, looking over every inch of the little cabin. "I feel like I'm in a dream."

"But it's true." He kissed her temple. "You're an amazing woman. Creighton wants you to have good things because the goodness in you has been shining through for years.

She blinked for a moment. "Oh. I'm not talking about the situation with Creighton. I'm talking about being here. With *you*." She lifted her fingers and pressed them over his lips before he could speak. "I'm talking about how much things have changed since I opened that envelope you sent me. The one with the very first key chain."

"It's been good, hasn't it?" Alex brushed his knuckles against the rosy glow of her cheek. "I've had a lot of fun watching you open the drawers. Spending time with you."

"I've changed," Yvette whispered. "And it's been good, but here's the part that feels like a dream." She looked straight into his eyes. "I'm in love with you."

Alex's brain buzzed as if he'd been hit on the head with a two-by-four.

He had no words. All the blood that would normally supply his brain with the ability to think and reason and talk had completely shut down.

The only thing still functioning was his heart, and the damn thing was pounding so hard, he swore the walls should be vibrating.

Yvette's serious expression turned into amusement. "Alex?"

He pulled her across his lap and into his arms and squeezed her so tight, he might've forced a squeak out of her. "Oh my God. Oh my *God*."

Laughter bubbled up, her torso rocking against his. "Not the reaction I expected, but I like it."

Somehow, he let her free far enough, he could cup her face in his hands. "Really? You love me?"

"That's what I'm going with, yeah. I've never felt like this before," she said, amusement draining away and seriousness returning. A lightness remained, bouncing between them and slipping out in her words. "I care about my friends, and I know what it feels like to want the best for people. But this thing inside that I feel for you? It's brand new. It feels precious, but not like a teacup or a delicate statue. It's the dogs racing around in the yard or finding a new batch of kittens. It's horses running in the springtime, kicking up their heels."

Trust the veterinarian to describe her emotions in such a way. So perfect for her.

Perfect for them.

He was still holding her. "I love you too. But I never dreamed this would happen."

"See? See what I mean? It's like a dream."

But it was the dream Alex had been hoping for from the beginning. "First kiss after saying *I love you*. This one should be extra sweet."

He put his lips to hers and took them softly.

She curled her arms around him, bodies coming into contact. Then she was tugging his T-shirt free and pulling it over his head. Stripping off her own top so they were skin to skin the next time their lips met.

Her words came out lusty and low, breath ghosting past his cheek as she played her fingers down his back. "Are we doing this here, or did you already put sheets on the bed?"

"Yes. And yes." It took a couple wiggles to get her straddling his legs, her jeans stripped away so she hovered close in just her bra and panties. Hands on her hips, he dragged her forward slowly over the thick ridge of his cock. "Damn, you feel good over me. "

"Would feel even better if you took everything off," she suggested, rocking her hips against him as little sounds escaped from the back of her throat. She stared into his eyes. "This is fun. And it's good, but I want it to be good for you too."

"I have a mostly naked woman in my arms who says she

loves me. I'm pretty much riding on a high right now," he confessed.

Still, he pushed her back far enough to scramble out of his own clothes. Yvette stopped in the middle of wiggling out of her panties, lifted her fingers to her mouth, and damn near giggled.

He glanced around. "What?"

She finished her task and crawled toward him, sliding her hand along his thigh—going the wrong direction. She patted his ankle and the thick wool socks still covering his feet. "You're such a cowboy."

THE MAN in front of her—buck naked except for the socks, flashed her an enormous grin then pulled her back into his lap. "I could get in so much trouble giving you a comeback to that line," Alex said.

A flashback to a time before, when she didn't understand why he was constantly teasing. To a time when she was a bit too sensitive and he was a little too brash.

But that was before, and this was now. "You did get in so much trouble, but I've figured out your brand of teasing."

"I don't want to give up *all* teasing. Especially not the kind that you like." Big, sturdy hands wrapped around her body. Fingertips drawing circles before sliding along her spine. Then he played with the sensitive skin at the top of her butt, grin growing wider the more she squirmed.

Every bit of her body was sensitized. Mentally, she urged his touch to travel. She wanted him to take hold again and squeeze her tight. To put their bodies in motion, sliding until they were no longer two separate units but one. That's what she wanted—

That's what she needed.

What Alex wanted too, but he seemed to be on a slow track

to the main event. Or at least a whole lot slower than Yvette hoped for right now.

It was time for a little encouragement of her own. She eased her hand along his thigh and stroked steadily higher. "You're a big fan of teasing, are you?"

A tortured gasp escaped him as she wrapped her fingers around his hard length. "Oh, hell yes."

Easy strokes, fingers tightening around the warm, silky heat. "So you don't mind if I do this for a while?"

Every muscle in his body had tightened. Head falling back, shaking gasps escaping his lips. "I want inside you. I want to be surrounded by your heat and held in your arms."

A shiver struck. Taunting him for longer would be fun, and yet she'd learned this lesson as well. Getting the thing you truly wanted was a special kind of joy.

Yvette snagged her abandoned jeans with her free hand and fished in the pocket for a condom. He groaned as she rolled it over him, fingers fumbling as excitement grew.

He cupped her ass as she knelt over him, her hand curled over his cock as she lifted then fell slowly, sliding together wickedly without slipping him into her sex. Nerves tingled; heat rose. The slick wetness from her body coated him.

"Yvette." He whispered her name.

She looked up as his tip notched between her folds. Their eyes met.

One slow, intimate glide, and they were joined. The pleasure in her body was matched by the joy in her heart—

His eyes. Oh, his *eyes* were so full of happiness and tenderness and love.

Truly, love.

She kissed him. "First kiss during sex after saying *I love you*."

"Making love," he corrected softly. "It's always making love between us."

Which set her heart fluttering even harder.

She lasted all of three minutes going slow. Then the sweet caress of his hands over her body plus the hungry nip of his teeth along her neck broke her. Yvette dug her fingers into his shoulders and rode him like a pony. Both of them gasping for air, small noises and grunts of pleasure stealing into the quiet of the cozy cabin.

Alex tightened his grip on her hips and held her high enough to pound up into her, her hand tucked between them as she stroked the place where they joined, teasing her clit.

They broke together, his loud growl echoing in her ear as he pulsed against her. Grunting again as her climax tightened around him.

She laughed, and he laughed, and they were kissing and holding each other so tight, there was nothing between them.

Nothing but love.

She was thankful to discover the cabin contained a surprisingly decadent bathroom, with a shower big enough for two. Which made cleaning up a little slower than usual but a lot more fun.

The day kept getting better. They worked together until a simple supper sat on the sturdy kitchen table. A meal that included crisp bacon and plenty of it.

Lots of talking still had to happen, but this was a good place to begin.

Only one concern still hung over her. Yvette waited until they'd finished eating and the small kitchen was tidied. Then she guided him back to the couch and took Alex's hand in hers. "There's one thing we need to talk about sooner than later."

"You're looking pretty serious."

"There's only one day left in the countdown chest." No matter how awkward, she had to have this conversation. "If we do spend the whole day up here, that means I won't open day twenty-four until Christmas Day."

Nothing untoward registered on his face.

"You have given me some amazing presents. Obviously, what you planned pretty much worked, because spending all that time together and getting to really know you made a difference."

"You're still looking worried," Alex said. "Now you're getting me riled up, and not in a good way."

Maybe it was better to just rip it off, Band-Aid style. "At one point I had to do a little surgery on the calendar chest. I dropped a key, and taking it apart was the only way, but when I got the key back, something else fell out."

She wiggled until she could slip it from her pocket. Because yes, she was still carrying it with her everywhere.

Obsessed, much?

She held up her hand, the ring resting in her palm.

Alex frowned, picking it up and examining it carefully. "Well, that's odd. I went over that chest from top to bottom when I was outfitting it with locks. Never the slightest idea there was something like this in it."

"So, it's not from you?"

His head snapped up, and he stared at her with enormous eyes. "Umm, no?"

She couldn't help it. A snort escaped. "That was definitive."

"I'm still wrapping my brain around this. It's a ring." He gasped. "Oh my God, it's a *ring*."

Yvette quivered with suppressed laughter. He'd echoed her first thoughts.

He shook his head. "Wow. I know I'm an optimistic son of a bitch, but even I find it difficult to imagine going from zero to ring in barely four weeks."

She let out a sigh, her spine melting with relief. "Thank God."

Alex lifted a brow. "The entire time, you thought I was about to propose? That must've been nerve-racking."

"Not the entire time. But yes, the last two weeks have been a little brain-tangling." She poked him in the chest. "I thought you were going to give me condoms way earlier than you did too, if you remember."

His grin was firmly back in place. "Sweetheart, that's a perfect lead-in. Remember, I said you got to set the pace. Frankly, I would be very happy to put that ring on your finger right now and slide into engagement town."

"Too soon," Yvette said quickly.

"Exactly."

"Not because I don't want to get there, maybe—but no, just no." Her face had to be flushed. She didn't want to make it sound as if she were rejecting *him*. "This is coming out all wrong."

Once again, she found herself in his lap, his strong arms around her. Fingers linked at the back of her head to direct her gaze straight on with his. "You said you love me. I don't *need* any other bells and whistles. Or rings, or bows." He lifted his free hand and teased a finger over her lips. "I do want to talk about what it means when two people discover they're in love. Where they live, how they spend their time. But I don't need any pretty trinket on your finger, or mine, to know that we belong together. Period."

Okay. Although a teasing moment of guilt did slide in and out faster than she thought possible. "Would it make you happy if we were engaged?"

His instant reaction was a light shrug. "Sure, but it doesn't have to be today." His smile widened again. "Also, I would like to be the one to give you a ring. Something we pick out together, instead of one you found lying around."

"Hidden away in the desk that has been in your family for years is *not* lying around," she said with mock seriousness." Then she leaned in and kissed him. Every bit of concern washed away. The goodness of his understanding made the warm spot inside grow again.

They sat there for a while, kissing and touching and talking about what might come next. They even went out on the porch, wrapped up from head to toe in blankets as they sat together and watched enormous snowflakes gently fall on the picturesque farm scene.

Alex used his phone to give them music, and this connection between them also felt right. They sang, his deeper tones a wonderful complement to her alto as they crooned "Winter Wonderland" and "White Christmas."

"It's a pretty place," Yvette said, fingers linked with Alex's under the covers. "It's got good bones."

"It's a fantastic place for you to set down roots."

That sounded sweet, but not quite right. Yvette repeated the words in her head. Definitely something she wanted to clear up. Diving into rings and talk of marriage—those were too soon. But she was one hundred percent sure of the feeling inside her heart.

She loved him. That part was rock solid, which meant this part needed to be crystal clear.

"For *us*," she corrected, meeting his gaze straight on. "This is where we can set down roots, together."

His smile could've lit up the countryside. "Together."

15

Their free day and a half out at the farm had been a little bit of heaven. Having to head into work on Christmas morning seemed a cruel punishment.

But first, they got to celebrate.

Far too bright and early, Yvette rolled on top of him in bed, bouncing like a little kid with excitement. "It's Christmas Day," she all but shouted. "Merry Christmas."

He rolled her under him, trying to ignore the time. "Merry Christmas. Sorry, there's nothing under the tree for you. Oh, wait. Maybe there is."

She blinked then all but threw him off, scrambling out of the chilly bedroom into the slightly warmer main room.

Laughter welled up as she settled on the floor beside the "tree" he'd pulled together last night, sneaking out of bed to get it set up. He'd lashed a branch from a spruce tree to one of the straight-backed kitchen chairs. Then he put her Christmas present on the seat of the chair, the package done up in shiny red paper with an enormous silver bow.

He joined her. "You do realize it's five in the morning."

"Which gives you just enough time to open your present

and still get to your shift on time." Yvette reached underneath the couch and pulled out a brightly wrapped package. "Ta-da. Here's part one."

It was Alex's turned to be amazed. "I knew ahead of time I was doing this, which is why I've got yours with me. You had my present with you in your truck?"

She looked sheepish. "I bought a present for Creighton and decided to get you a set as well. Your real present is something else. You get it later today."

He dropped to the floor beside her. "Well, Merry Christmas to us."

Paper flew. A lot of paper, because Alex had wrapped Yvette's gift in five separate layers, just to make her smile.

Her gift to him turned out to be a set of sheepskin-lined work gloves. Sturdy and warm. "I love them." He slipped them on, and they fit perfectly. "You knew the right size."

She paused as she placed a finally unwrapped photo album in her lap. "I've had your hands all over me enough for the past month. I knew what size to get."

Amusement shot to high. Alex pressed the soft leather over her breasts. "Please, tell me you did this in the middle of the store."

She outright snickered.

He blinked, hands falling away in surprise. "You *did*?"

Yvette lifted her fingers to her mouth. "I told you, I wanted to get the right size."

She was blooming in so many wonderful ways. "I wish I'd been there to see it."

Yvette flipped open the first page of the photo album, her mouth opening in awe. "Oh, Alex. I love it."

"Your friends helped. Hanna and the rest. They were sneaky for me, taking pictures and looking back in time for extra shots."

Twenty-four days of pictures. Not just from this December,

but some from *the time before*. When the two of them had still been at odds but drawn together repeatedly by common friends and their work.

He'd taken a picture of every single key chain and put that image in the top corner. The rest of the page was them. Places they'd been, situations they'd dealt with that fit the theme of the day.

Day two, and the star key chain was accompanied by a shot from Silver Stone two years earlier. A tiny foal with a starlike marking on its forehead that Yvette had helped deliver.

Day fourteen was a candle. The picture next to it was one Brooke had snapped the night they'd had the bonfire, with firelight glow dancing on their faces as Alex leaned across to kiss her.

The image of them in their award-winning ugly sweaters surrounded by mutated snowmen. A picture of them on horses. Of them at the fire hall with their friends, her giving him side-eye as he made a funny face.

All of it was there. A record of connection and growing unity.

She looked up, and her eyes sparkled. "You left a lot of empty pages."

"New memories. They'll be coming," he assured her.

She squeezed him tight, damn near mashing them together. Alex somehow dragged himself out the door on time and headed off down the snowy drive feeling as if he were twenty feet tall.

His entire—thankfully short—work shift was a blur, and he raced his way across to the seniors' lodge to meet up with Yvette as promised. They walked together from the parking lot hand in hand.

The first surprise was discovering Creighton sitting outside the front door on one of the wide benches that faced toward the mountain view. Tex sat at his feet, tail thumping as they approached.

"Merry Christmas," Alex offered.

"Bah, humbug." But Creighton grinned. "You too."

Yvette stopped a foot in front of Creighton. She leaned down and spoke softly. "Merry Christmas."

The next moment, she'd wrapped her arms around him, hugging him. The old man's eyes widened in shock, but he lifted his arms and squeezed her tight. His eyes closed as happiness rolled over his weathered face.

"Stuff and nonsense, you know." The words came out gruff and grumpy.

He forced a frown as she stood and folded her arms, mischief in her eyes. "Happy holidays? We're too late for joyous Solstice."

Creighton waved a hand. "Fine. Merry Christmas. How are my dogs?"

"Happy. Warm. Missing you, though. They told me themselves before we left that they hope you come to visit sometime." She shook her head, smile softening. "We'll talk more about your generous offer, but thank you. I have a lot to think about."

"It's the holidays." He frowned at Alex. "Why is she talking business when it's the holidays? You aren't making the day very festive for her."

"You're right," Alex said, passing Yvette the bag with Creighton's present before holding out the one he'd gotten the man. "Time to celebrate. Hurry up, old man. I hear there's cake happening soon, and I don't want to miss it."

A snort of amusement escaped Creighton. He unwrapped the pair of slippers Alex had gotten him, and the gloves from Yvette, his stern face suddenly a lot older and more fragile.

He met Yvette's gaze and sighed. "Thanks for being kind to an *old man*. Now get. You can come see me next week and tell me how much you're going to pay me and how you're going to fix up my place."

"It was not a problem to be kind to you," Yvette insisted. Her nose wrinkled before she added, "Well, mostly it wasn't a problem."

Creighton full-on laughed. Then he turned to Alex. "Just so you know, you were right. That road to my place is a pain in the ass. I put it that way to annoy the hell out of a good friend of mine. He lost a bet, and so I got to build my access road straight through the middle of one of his grazing sections, just to make him cuss me out every damn time he moved cattle."

Good grief. "Seriously?"

"He's dead now, so there's no fun in it anymore." The older man nodded, an evil glint in his eye. "There's another right of way onto the property, just off Highway 34. Figured you could make a road through the trees on the east section and cut the drive time from town to under 10 minutes."

"You're a bad one," Yvette offered.

He shrugged. "A man's got to enjoy life however he can."

Yvette was still shaking her head and laughing as they left Creighton and Tex to join the rest of the party.

The inside of the lodge was full of holiday scents and sounds. Alex kept his fingers curled around Yvette's as they made their way into the secure wing.

Before they joined her grandparents, Alex pulled Yvette aside and brought out his phone. He held it forward, the song he'd lined up visible on the screen. "You okay singing this as a present for your grandparents?"

Her smile was blinding. "I love you."

He winked. "I'll take that as a yes."

Sweet happiness followed as hugs were exchanged. Yvette's grandfather continued to smile and nod as presents were unwrapped, although he didn't want to unwrap any himself. Grandma Geraldine hummed happily as she watched her friends interact with their great-grandchildren. "It's a good day."

Yvette waited until the excitement and wrapping paper had finished flying. "Grandma. We have something else for you."

She nodded at Alex, and he pulled her to her feet. Music playing, he took her by the hand and together, they sang "Have Yourself a Merry Little Christmas."

He wasn't a performer, and this wasn't a performance where making eye contact with the audience was important. Maybe he should have done a little more, but the only person he had eyes for was Yvette. She was the only person who could truly make this holiday feeling inside him last throughout the entire year.

They finished singing, and he pulled her into his arms, the seniors in the room clapping and nodding. Grandma Geraldine wiped at her eyes.

But it was Yvette's grandfather who gave Alex the biggest kick. His expression was pure joy as he looked Alex in the eye and winked.

Hugs and kisses finished, Alex and Yvette made it back to her place shortly before four o'clock. The timing was pretty perfect, considering they wouldn't need to start cooking anything for a while.

However could they spend their time?

"So, what's my second present?" Alex teased, sliding an arm around her waist and nuzzling his lips below her ear. "Does it involve card games? Nudity? Both?"

"All wonderful ideas, and I'll keep track of those for next time, but none of the above. I still think you'll like it." She took a deep breath then wiggled her phone in the air. "We're talking with your parents. They should be calling in a few minutes."

~

His face—

Yvette could stare at it forever. Or snap a picture and put it in the dictionary under the word *astonished*.

"My *parents*?" Alex swallowed. "You talked to them?" He didn't sound upset but downright gleeful.

"I know how important they are to you, and I wanted a chance to meet them, so to speak. You and I had arranged to spend the rest of the day together, and I was worried you wouldn't get a chance to connect with them."

He tugged her fingers to his lips and kissed them. "I want to —jeez, I have no words. *Again*. Ms. Wright, you're batting a thousand when it comes to saying things that tip me right off my feet."

"You're okay that I called them without you knowing?"

"Hell yes." He leaned in, eyes dancing with mischief. "Tell me my dad said something to embarrass himself."

She laughed. "They were very nice. We didn't talk for long. Just made plans for them to FaceTime with us."

There wasn't time for nervousness to rise, because her phone was ringing. The next thing she knew, Alex had tucked his arm around her and taken control of the screen. He dropped it into an empty glass on the table, propping it up so the screen showed the two of them all curled up and cozy.

On the other side of the screen, a far larger group than two appeared.

"Merry Christmas." The chorus rang out from the crowd, and Yvette smiled, gaze dancing over the gathering. She waved back at a little girl sitting in the lap of a silver-haired man on the couch.

Alex answered for them both. "Merry Christmas. This is a surprise. Cait, Aaron. You found some Christmas elves?"

Everyone in the Thorne household was wearing a bright-green sweater. Neon bright, with big red bows across the chest.

"Hey, Alex. Hi, Yvette. Nice to meet you. That's Davis. I'm

Caitlin, this is my husband, Aaron. We've got Thomas, Tisha, and Nyx celebrating with us this year."

"I'm Nyx," the youngest announced, squirming in place. "Why aren't you wearing funny sweaters?"

"I don't know. We should do something about that, shouldn't we, Alex?" Yvette pointed at the little girl. "You wait right there. I'll be back."

Without thinking, she pressed a quick kiss to Alex's cheek then rose to grab their sweaters. A chorus of catcalls and whistles carried over the phone.

Alex took the teasing with humour, jibbing back at his older brother. Yvette slipped on her sweater then modeled it, pushing Alex's hands off when he tried to demonstrate how the Velcro animals worked.

Laughter rang out again and again. Nyx and her siblings showed off the presents they'd gotten, and the visit was sweet and special, and Yvette couldn't have imagined anything better.

When Cait and Aaron slipped their family away, though, leaving just Hans and Glenda, Yvette's cheeks heated all over again.

"We won't keep you much longer, but has it been a good holiday season?" Glenda asked.

"It's been—" How to describe what had happened? How to share the changes Yvette felt inside after all she'd learned and experienced this month?

She glanced at Alex. He was no help. He was staring at her with love in his eyes.

She turned back to his parents. Their expressions were full of kindness, but they were clearly amused as well. Good people, who had raised a wonderful son.

Whom she loved.

"Your son is very special. Thank you for sharing him with me."

Hans grinned. "You want to keep him?"

"*Dad*," Alex complained. "I just spent a month getting her to stop running away. Don't scare her—"

"Yes," Yvette interrupted. She curled her arm around his. "I'm keeping him. I hope you don't mind."

Glenda clapped her hands together, face full of delight. "Really?"

"Does this mean wedding plans?" Hans asked.

Yvette shivered. Wordless for a moment.

"Not yet," Alex said, beaming at her. "When she's ready."

"You should have put it on the list, son." Hans teased. "But that's just fine. It's clear you two are meant for each other. We don't need any special ceremony to make that true."

"We look forward to more visits," Glenda said, her smile bright, the words gentle. "And you go right ahead and call me anytime you want, Yvette. I love visits and phone calls and hearing how wonderful my son is. Or how he's messed up— that's also fun to hear, if you need to grumble for a bit."

Yvette laughed. A memory cut in. "Oh. To change the topic for a moment. You know the present Alex gave me this year? The desk with daily presents?""

"I helped with the locks," Hans said proudly. "But it was all his idea."

"It was a wonderful idea, and I really enjoyed it. But there's also a mystery to solve." The sensation inside was now sheer curiosity. No worry, no concern. She once again pulled the ring from her pocket and lifted it up to view. "I found this, and Alex said he has no idea—"

"Oh my goodness." Glenda was halfway to her feet in shock.

She dropped back into her chair, turning to Hans with her mouth hanging open. "You really did—I mean, is *that* the ring?"

Hans laughed. A huge sound that rolled up from his belly as he pulled his wife into his arms and squeezed her tight. "I told you I'd gotten you a ring. I *told* you."

Yvette glanced at Alex.

He lifted his shoulders in an easy shrug. "No idea what's going on. Mom, Dad. Stop smooching and spill the beans. Whose ring is this?" he demanded.

Because his parents were kissing. Rather vigorously, in fact, and Yvette found herself grinning hard as Glenda finally pushed Hans back far enough so they could both once again look into the camera.

"Once upon a time, *that* was my writing desk. Hans told me he'd left me a present on it, and I—well, I had a slight mishap and bumped into it when I ran to see. I found a flower and some chocolate. Both of which I enjoyed very much and said thank you for. But when I never mentioned the ring, he thought I was ignoring him—"

"Damn woman not only told me there was no ring, but that if I thought I could propose without one, I had another think coming." Hans grinned again. "We got some good mileage out of that fight, I'm telling you."

"This was supposed to be your engagement ring?" Yvette carefully curled her fingers around it. "I'll put it somewhere safe for you. I'm glad we found it."

"I'm glad too. Of course, if Alex wants it, I don't mind sharing..." Glenda waggled her brows suggestively then laughed again. "I'll stop. You two set your own pace."

"But she's serious," Hans whispered. "Never doubt that."

"I've got it covered," Alex told them with dry amusement.

Children laughed in the background, and Yvette let the happiness of the moment flow through her as she held Alex's hand. "We'd love to chat some more, but we should let you get back to your family."

"You *are* family," Glenda said smoothly. "Welcome, Yvette. Alex, we love you. You two enjoy the rest of the holidays."

"Love you too. Chat soon," Alex promised.

It was all Yvette could do to keep a smile in place until the call cut off and she could safely bury her face against Alex's neck. His strong arms wrapped around her and held her as, once again, tears fell.

"I'm not this weepy all the time," she insisted when the tearing jag faded.

"Never apologize for letting your feelings show." He wiped away a tear of his own. "They're real family. You have people who love you. Never doubt that."

They ended up at Brooke and Mack's for a couple of hours, all their group gathered around the firepit in the backyard. The temperature was just below freezing, and the warmth of friends was nearly as strong as the fire's glow.

They all sang happy birthday to Talia, then she and Crissy went to make snow angels in the backyard, their dads helping as required. Brooke eased forward in her seat so she could talk to Yvette around Hanna, who held her sleeping two-year-old in her arms. Madison stared into the fire with a Madonna-like smile on her face, having been bundled up by Ryan and their daughter before the kids took off to play.

It was a gathering full of happiness and warmth.

Yvette's entire day had been bursting with joy from the first minute she'd rolled over and seen Alex's eyes. Seen the love in them.

A couple hours later, they were back at Yvette's, curling up in front of the fire. She wasn't sure her heart could hold much more.

Only, she was curious about one thing. Her magpie nature had heard a shiny comment, and now she wanted to know more.

She linked her fingers with Alex's. "Can I ask you something?"

"Anything."

"Your dad said something about *adding it to the list*." Yvette gestured. "This afternoon when we chatted."

His expression grew serious. "I did some hard thinking

when I left here last spring. I'd figured out we belonged together, but making it happen still needed work. So I made a list."

She frowned. "You made a countdown calendar."

"Yes, but first I made a list." He pulled a card from his pocket and held it out to her. Tidy handwriting, the edges of the paper well worn.

She's got a generous heart, but she's tender as well. Be kind, be giving.
Let her give back.
She likes shiny things, surprises.
She won't want expensive gifts but thoughtful ones.
She needs to be listened to.
She needs a man as honest and trustworthy as she is.
She needs to know how much I appreciate her skills and her opinion.
She needs to see what's important to me by what I do—and that
means:
She needs to know she's important to me by how I treat her.
So stop being an ass!

Yvette pressed a hand to his cheek. "You're amazing."

"So are you. Which is why I made the list." He twisted his head until he could kiss her palm. "You still have one drawer to open. We weren't here for day twenty-four."

Since she didn't need to worry about finding an empty space where she'd thought the ring she'd found belonged, Yvette's enthusiasm shot to high. "I'm going to be really sad now that the holidays are over. I like having secrets to open."

His grin seemed far too bright. "Hurry up. Let's go."

Standing on the porch, twenty-five days after starting this adventure, it felt as if far more time had passed. As if Alex standing at her side, fingers linked, was how they'd always been.

The final key ring was a rainbow. The key itself was bright

blue. Yvette surveyed the drawers, trying to remember which one she hadn't opened yet.

One of the smallest drawers under the rolltop had a blue lock.

"I see it." Yvette hurried to open the drawer, humming happily as she discovered another charm for her bracelet. "A rainbow. Oh, Alex, I love it."

She picked it up, pausing as paper ruffled.

An envelope lay at the bottom of the drawer.

Alex's expression was mischief and happiness. "Merry Christmas."

"What's this?" She ripped the envelope open and gasped. "Another key?"

"Well, you did say you were sad you didn't have any more secrets to look forward to."

Oh no. "What does it open?" Yvette asked, suspicion rising.

"A secret that you'll receive in a month or so." Alex held up his hands as if he were a magician. "Ta-da. You now have something to look forward to."

She was going to kill him. Or kiss him. One of those two. "You are terrible, and wonderful, and so terribly wonderful that I'm going to have to keep a close eye on you from now on."

"Fine with me." Alex breathed out a happy sigh, pulling her into his arms and holding her tight.

The mystery key in her fingers sent the right kind of excitement through her. The warmth of his body, the right kind of connection.

The look in his eyes, the perfect kind of love.

Yvette kissed her cowboy, so grateful he'd been willing to make his list. To work to bring them from their past into what she was certain would be a wonderful future. One precious day at a time.

EPILOGUE

Jan 1, Heart Falls

Quiet hung on the air in the empty church, a still, solemn hush broken only by the faint sound of wind whistling against the tall steeple. Sunlight streamed in the stained-glass windows, sending brightly coloured patches dancing down the aisle all the way to where Ashton Stewart stood.

Dressed in his best suit with polished boots and his hair combed back as neatly as it ever got, he would've felt like a fool except for the pounding in his heart.

He glanced at his watch. Three minutes to noon.

Three more minutes to wait.

Such a short time to wait to discover if he'd finally figured out the truth that would stop his heart from breaking.

Three minutes until Sonora arrived.

Or didn't—

New York Times Bestselling Author Vivian Arend
invites you to Heart Falls. These contemporary ranchers live in
a tiny town in central Alberta, tucked into the rolling foothills.
Enjoy the ride as they each find their happily-ever-afters.

Holidays at Heart Falls
A Firefighter's Christmas Gift
A Soldier's Christmas Wish
A Hero's Christmas Hope
A Cowboy's Christmas List
A Rancher's Christmas Kiss

The Stones of Heart Falls
A Rancher's Heart
A Rancher's Song
A Rancher's Bride
A Rancher's Love
A Rancher's Vow

The Colemans of Heart Falls
The Cowgirl's Forever Love
The Cowgirl's Secret Love
The Cowgirl's Chosen Love

ABOUT THE AUTHOR

With over 2.5 million books sold, Vivian Arend is a *New York Times* and *USA Today* bestselling author of over 60 contemporary and paranormal romance books, including the Six Pack Ranch and Granite Lake Wolves.

Her books are all standalone reads with no cliffhangers. They're humorous yet emotional, with sexy-times and happily-ever-afters. Vivian pretty much thinks she's got the best job in the world, and she's looking forward to giving readers more HEAs. She lives in B.C. Canada with her husband of many years and a fluffy attack Shih-tzu named Luna who ignores everyone except when treats are deployed.

www.vivianarend.com

$15-

9 781989 507407